About

Ryan left Newcastle University in 2013, graduating with a first-class BA in history. Soon after he became the editor of AltFi.com, now one of the leading news and analysis resources for 'fintech' in the UK. This role has given him a ringside seat from which to observe the rise of the alternative finance industry, which spans crowdfunding, peer-to-peer lending, digital banking and robo-advice, and which is one of the hottest niches in disruptive technology globally.

When not writing, Ryan will likely be working on his podcast (*Millennial Money Matters*) or consuming or participating in some variety of sport. *Pimple* is his first novel.

PIMPLE

Live, love, laugh, Laura,

Bulll

PIMPLE

RYAN WEEKS

This edition first published in 2018

Unbound

6th Floor Mutual House, 70 Conduit Street, London W1S 2GF

www.unbound.com

© Ryan Weeks, 2018

ISBN (eBook): 978-1911586814

ISBN (Paperback): 978-1911586807

Design by Mecob

Cover image:

© Shutterstock.com / sakkmesterke

FSC
www.fsc.org

MIX
Paper from
responsible sources
FSC® C018072

Printed in Great Britain by Clays Ltd, St Ives plc

For Rebecca. I have pondered at great length how to phrase this, and am not content simply to say that words, such as I know them, are not up to the task. My best attempt is to say that I want for all the finest things I do in life to be tied irrevocably to you – as is my heart.

Dear Reader,

The book you are holding came about in a rather different way to most others. It was funded directly by readers through a new website: Unbound.

Unbound is the creation of three writers. We started the company because we believed there had to be a better deal for both writers and readers. On the Unbound website, authors share the ideas for the books they want to write directly with readers. If enough of you support the book by pledging for it in advance, we produce a beautifully bound special subscribers' edition and distribute a regular edition and e-book wherever books are sold, in shops and online.

This new way of publishing is actually a very old idea (Samuel Johnson funded his dictionary this way). We're just using the internet to build each writer a network of patrons. Here, at the back of this book, you'll find the names of all the people who made it happen.

Publishing in this way means readers are no longer just passive consumers of the books they buy, and authors are free to write the books they really want. They get a much fairer return too – half the profits their books generate, rather than a tiny percentage of the cover price.

If you're not yet a subscriber, we hope that you'll want to join our publishing revolution and have your name listed in one of our books in the future. To get you started, here is a £5 discount on your first pledge. Just visit unbound.com, make your pledge and type PIMPLE18 in the promo code box when you check out.

Thank you for your support,

Dan, Justin and John
Founders, Unbound

Super Patrons

Carol Allison
Andy Allison
Ian Anderson
John Andrews
David Andrews
Michael Aylwin
Sue Baker
Michael Baptista
Chloe Barlass
Peter Becker
Chris Bellringer
Jack Billings
Susan Billings
Aldwyn Boscawen
Nicholas Brown
Fifi Bullard-weeks
Martin Campbell
Angus Campbell
Rick Challener
Mark Colley
Mike Colley
Philip Cramp
Caroline Crawford
Ben Davisson
Tom Dawe
Stephan Demoulin
Terry Duffy
Rory Dunnett
Robert Ede
Alix Eakins
Robert Edmonds
Richard Emms
Joe Faddoul
Christian Faes
Aloysius Fekete
Alessandro Ferrario
Michael Fine

Andrew Gill
Daniel Godfrey
Nick Gregory
Sam Griffiths
Manuel Guerrero
Sue Hainsby
Hugh Halford-Thompson
Melanie Haworth
Jemima Hindle
Abigail Howard
Fiona Hurlock
Gosia Jalowiecka
Martyn James
Jenny Jeffs
Mike Jessop
Darren Johns
Jason Kennard
Derek Kenny
Dan Kieran
William King
Tyron King
Senthil Kumarathevan
Ian Lansdell
Howie Li
Jo Lingard
Alexander Lyne
Harry Lynn
Seonaid Mackenzie-Murray
Jamie Macrae
Roberta Main-Millar
Paul & Julia McMenemy
Tom Mitchell
John Mitchinson
Isabell Moessler
Joe Murley
Matthew Newman
Kwaku Osei-Afrifa
Alison & Rob Ovens
Matthew Parkin
Justin Pollard
Ben Ransom

A Reader
Lucy Reynolds
Sam Ridley
Christopher Roche
Carl Rogers
Martin Rutland
Lynsey Searle
Barry Sinfield
Tim Smith
Darren Spears
David Stevenson
Fiona Swain
Jimmy Sykes
Rupert Taylor
Steve Thomas
Grant Thompson
Jamie Tittle
Goncalo de Vasconcelos
Rebecca Warner
Mark Weeks
Sam Weeks
Maureen Weeks
Gemma Weeks
Huw Williams
Peter Wilson
Caroline Winn
Hugo Winn

With grateful thanks to Mark Weeks, who helped make this book happen.

Contents

Part I. L'Ancien Régime

1. In Remembrance of Flowery Shirts 21
2. Secret Victories 31
3. Go 37
4. Sacrifice 45
5. The Incumbent 49
6. Beta Testing 55
7. The Fruitless To-and-Fro 63
8. Beyond Deference 69
9. Customer Acquisition 75

Part II. Revolution

10. Virgin Clients 85
11. The Knightsbridge Parlour 101
12. UX 109
13. Misgivings 117

Part III. Restoration

14. The Founding of the Fist 129
15. Gold Rush 133
16. The Wild Horse 137
17. Tim Nestler 141
18. In the Media 145
19. Brunch and Murder 149
20. Bicyclists and Breakups 153
21. Taking a Stand 157
22. The Mural 161

23. A Name to Hang a Case Around   165
24. The Leech   169
25. Collapse   173
26. A Drunken Eureka   175

Part IV. Enlightenment

27. The Tower   181

Acknowledgements   203
Patrons   205
Teaser Chapter   207

PART I

L'Ancien Régime

1

In Remembrance of Flowery Shirts

There were five advertisements on the wall across from Annie: for Uber, for Airbnb, for TaskRabbit, for Deliveroo and finally for Zopa. Transport, accommodation, labour, food and finance, each arisen into the technological age. *Whatever next?* she wondered.

Soporific light warped in and out of the Tube windows. The carriage flickered to the tune of a faulty bulb. None of the passengers were speaking, nor interacting in any way. Breaths were drawn roughly. Staccato thumbs bounced upon keypads. Bums and shoes shuffled. Throats were cleared and recleared of some persistent blockage.

The distance that for now separated Annie from the conference ahead was rapidly eroding. The air around her felt very close, as the Tube rattled out of the deep blue afternoon and into the sudden darkness of a tunnel. The bodies of the people nearby perturbed her. Everything around her felt abrupt, loud and overbearing. She felt the heat acutely too. Sweat began to creep between her skin and the inner lining of her grey duffle coat, and to cling lightly to the border of her freckled forehead and her wild, curly head of hair.

Southwark. Not far to go now. She closed her eyes and lowered her head a little to hide the twitching of her voiceless lips.

Ladies and gentlemen, thank you so much for inviting me to speak this evening, her thoughts began. She summoned up a vision of the lectern. My name is Annie O'Mahony. *I am the original founder – since departed – of Millennial Credit, or MILC, as many of you will no doubt know it from those god-awful commercials.*

The corners of her lips curled – a moment's respite from her anxiety. For such a long time she had felt nothing but bitterness at the mention of the company. Yet here she was, poised to deliver a sermon on its origins, and on the origins of an industry that she had tried so desperately to forget.

'We will shortly be arriving at London Bridge,' declared the announcement system, the familiar and peculiar pause between 'at' and 'London' prompting Annie's hands to shake upon her thighs.

Stop it, she demanded of herself. And sure enough, the shaking stopped. She felt better today than she had done in months, but a latent fear lurked deep within her stomach – fear that regression would swallow her whole. She strode into the crisp air. Her heels click-clacked upon the cobbled stones of Borough Market. People seemed to leer as she passed by.

Annie soon stood on the front steps of the crumbling old brewery. Phantoms of memory flowed in and out of the grand glass doors. Soon their faces would regain life. Not wanting to dwell a second longer on what awaited her, she slipped into the hallways of the complex.

A low, rumbling drone of human activity greeted her, but before she had time to unpick the cacophony, a stout and slick gentleman approached, poised to make an introduction.

'Mrs O'Mahony?' he ventured.

'It's Miss, actually.'

'My apologies, Miss O'Mahony.'

'Not to worry. In truth, I prefer Annie. And you are?'

'Annie it is!' he exclaimed, extending her a bulbous palm. 'Henry Troupe. I'm one of the directors here at DisTech.'

DisTech stood for disruptive technology – a media group that Annie knew well. It had thrown together the industry's first conference, back in the early days of Millennial Credit. It was something of a custom for disruptive technology companies to abbreviate words or syllables and then to attach them to one another. Social Finance, for example, had become SoFi. It was only natural that DisTech, as an industry news site, had followed suit.

Already Annie could taste the shift in dynamic. There had been no foreboding rumble at the entrance to that inaugural and humble affair of five years past. Nor had there been a Henry Troupe, draped in his drab dark suit, sporting a brightly coloured tie: a sickly orange tie, his best attempt at vibrancy.

They passed together into the belly of the building. Pockets of whisperers soon became crowds of speakers and listeners. Mostly deaf to Henry's small talk, Annie descended as if into a dream. The once warren-like wine-makers had been bombarded with paint and chisel. The old bare-brick walls that used to quake and crumble at the passing of trains overhead had been flattened, smoothed and painted vanilla.

Soon she began to pick up on the old snippets of jargon. A 'disin-termediation', a couple of 'USPs', the odd 'start-up culture', multiple references to the industry as a 'space', rather than as a sector. She even overheard one woman saying 'squaring the circle', and was forced to stifle a laugh.

There was one particularly distinctive set of attendees, each wearing a bizarrely out-of-place kind of sports jacket. The jackets were bright red, made of a lightweight waterproof material, and emblazoned with the Lending Cube logo.

The founder of the Lending Cube was a keen sailor, and an old rival of Annie's. He had broken a number of speed records in a niche field of sailing in which the swiftness of a yacht is largely a measure of the money that has been spent on it. Annie considered the jackets as much a tip to his achievements as a bid for industry omnipotence.

The time for observation was all but over. For now, Mr Troupe's part – inane as it was – appeared to be coming to an anticlimactic close. Annie was being passed over to the care of a familiar figure: David Leighton, who had pulled together the original DisTech industry bash. He was a messy-by-design, kindly sort of character, and he beamed as he planted a kiss on either side of Annie's densely freckled face. He then held her by the shoul-ders for a moment before flopping his arms to his sides.

'How are you, Annie?'

'All the better for seeing that you're still lumbering around, Mr Leighton!' Annie chuckled.

He laughed his hearty laugh, his body wobbling in accompani-ment. He looked older, by her estimation, and somewhat wearied behind the cheerful film of his hazel eyes.

'You'll note that I've been stripped of my flowery shirts.' He looked as though he might risk a nudge.

'The bastards,' Annie whispered, loudly.

'Hey ho,' replied David. 'Now, I presume you've been suitably briefed?'

Together they were progressing along a corridor that flanked what appeared to be the main conference space.

'I have. Not to worry.'

'Any nerves?' he asked, being sure to avoid eye contact.

'Ha! None whatsoever,' came the reply, a tad too quickly.

They were now standing in the wings of a broad-based stage, on which a tremendous digital screen formed a backdrop that would soon display Annie's every movement. The screen itself was lodged like a jewel into a great blanched canvas, which bore the words *DisTech Summit 2016*. There was a plethora of sponsor logos, most of which would be illegible to anyone beyond the front rows.

The previous presenter had offered up a staggeringly grandiose presentation in which he had likened the ascent of his company to the course of the French Revolution. He began with 'L'Ancien Régime' – the backward times of bank monopoly. Next came 'Revolution' – the emergence of a digital alternative. Then the 'Restoration' – during which the banks bit back. And finally, 'Enlightenment' – which was yet to come to pass.

'Good luck up there, Annie,' said David. 'We really must catch up some time soon. Been far too long.'

Annie allowed the statement to hang in the air a moment. 'We must,' she replied, suspecting the old man of insincerity. They hadn't caught up in years. 'Thank you, David.'

With an awkward convulsion of the neck, the DisTech orchestrator shuffled away, leaving Annie to await the echo of her own name.

When it came, she breathed as deeply as she could. She drove her fingertips into her palms. She fastened her eyes shut, and, as she reopened them, strained to relax her every sinew, to loosen her joints and untangle her thoughts. She strode onto the stage, purposely planting each pace. She wore a toothy smile, and tried to convey keenness and liveliness in her wandering blue eyes.

She played pleasantries with her introducer, kissing him on each cheek before dismissing him stage left and taking her place at the lectern. The applause began to subside – a camouflaged, orchestral melody that became more noticeable with each retiring instrument. The glare of the spotlight also began to wane, and beyond it faces were sizzling into view. There were a great many more men than there were women.

'Ladies and gentlemen, thank you so much for inviting me to speak this evening. My name is Annie O'Mahony, and I am the original founder – since departed – of Millennial Credit.'

She paused, and leaped ahead a sentence or so in her mind, setting herself down on the safe side of the joke which she feared, if received poorly, might sweep her composure away. She became conscious of moderating her Northern Irish twang, which was often more pronounced the more impassioned she became.

'I have been asked to talk to you not about where the peer-to-peer lending industry is, nor about where it is headed, but rather about where it was born, and indeed why it was born. The short version is that it boiled down to two requirements, and one overarching principle. Requirement number one' – she raised a single, slender finger to the rafters –'was the need to supply finance to the underserved, on reasonable terms, at faster speeds than incumbent providers could match. Requirement number two was the need to provide a better deal to individual investors.' She paused again in an attempt to disperse the static that seemed to cluster about her the longer she went uninterrupted.

'The principle was that each need could eradicate the other, using the connective power of that wonderful thing we call the World Wide Web. Back in 2006, and to a certain extent still, finance was one of the last bastions of physical infrastructure. Other industries – music, video, travel and commerce – had each fallen to technological advancement. But finance, perplexingly, just hadn't experienced that same shift. Our mission was to change that.'

And so she trundled onwards, sticking to her remit, staying the course – offering up musings on origins, and on origins alone. It was a long, hieroglyphic portrayal of a now – by her estimation at least – grossly mutated thing.

The speech drew to a close. The applause was rapturous. The moderator's thanks were flamboyant. Annie was humble in her reception of both. But before she could escape the clutches of the crowd, a call for questions was sounded.

She had been blindsided. There had been no mention of 'Q and A'. In the periphery of her vision she glimpsed a table of dourly dressed men, whose slack collective form had snapped suddenly erect. It was Millennial Credit's board of directors, and they were clearly panicked by the compere's slip-up. But there was no turning back now. The hands were already raised. The microphones were roaming.

'You at the back. The gentleman in the pink.' There was very little pink out there in that rippling sea of grey and black.

'Jason Henderson, *Online Chronicle*.' Preliminaries of this kind were textbook. 'You spoke of the social impact of peer-to-peer lending. Does peer-to-peer today – if you can still call it that – retain any social value, given the high level of institutional involvement?'

The rippling crowd turned tumultuous. There was light laughter, muttering and misgivings. Annie was reeling. The game had changed. No longer was she being asked to recycle parts of a well-remembered past, but rather to opine upon the present. And her opinions upon this particular subject were widely known. Hence the question, she later supposed.

'Annie O'Mahony. Unemployed,' she began, her mouth twisting slowly into a smile. Laughter came mercifully from the audience. Never had she strained so hard to do so little. 'It's still a better deal for both sides.' The stage had a hold of her, and wouldn't let go until she offered up at least a sliver of her true self. 'Just about,' she added, with a flash of cheek and excitement.

Chuckling bubbled up again in several pockets of the audience, while the spaces between them seemed to darken, like landmasses emerging from the sea. The suddenly stiff compere felt for his earlobe.

'Ladies and gentlemen,' he said, oozing counterfeit regret. 'I'm afraid to say that's all we have time for. Please join me in a rousing round of applause for Miss Annie O'Mahony. She's been brilliant.'

The orchestra of hands plucked up its tune once more. The numbing effect, not just on the ears but on all the senses, returned. Annie floated from the stage and away from the thousand eyes of the crowd.

Relief filled her from the ground upwards. She had weathered a public appearance, and with scarcely so much as an emotional palpitation. The feat felt like the final footfall in a long and arduous climb – not to a great height, but into the open air, from deep within a shadowy and haunted chasm. She had embraced, if not quite endorsed, the status quo – for all to see.

Her frame felt loose and unencumbered. She soon found herself embroiled in an endless string of reintroductions. She reminisced with ex-colleagues and laughed with old friends. She probed for industry gossip. She offered flirtatious jibes to bankers.

The final day of this 48-hour slog of a conference was now disintegrating into an extravagant drinks reception. Spindly men bore silver platters of wine between the slackening delegates. Annie couldn't resist chancing one. Soon enough she had chanced a few.

Trays of canapés were wheeled between the bodies. The tray-lanes gradually broadened as more and more people slipped away into the evening. Industry awards were being handed out in the background, but nobody seemed to be paying them much attention – save, of course, for the people who had paid to win.

Annie stood entertaining a trio of dull men. The feeling of release had given way to a slight tipsiness, and the transition had been too subtle for her to notice. Lips were looser. A tall and burly man in a great grey suit joined the company, looming into view from a nearby corner. Voices rushed to introduce him.

'Annie, this is Rory de Sansa.'

'Oh, I know who this is,' said Annie, smiling and extending a cool palm. 'And how are we, Mr de Sansa?'

'Quite well, Miss O'Mahony, thank you.' The board was set; a war of subtext was about to begin.

'Tell me of today's MILC,' she exclaimed, with a touch more gusto than intended.

'I'm glad you asked,' he beamed, dipping his head down to her level. 'Well you'll have heard, I'm sure, that we've just passed the £5 billion mark.'

'Most impressive!' she returned.

'Still a fair way behind the Yanks, but significant progress.'

'Oh Rory,' said Annie, touching him on the arm. 'I do so hope you're growing sensibly.' She was a vision of concern.

He smiled a sickly-sweet smile. 'We're regulated now, Annie. We're required to be.'

Annie checked herself, determined not to shatter the indifferent display she had put on up to now. 'Well I'm pleased to hear it,' she said, straining to keep each syllable smoothly connected to the next.

'We'll let the Q one numbers do the talking, I suppose!' said de Sansa.

Annie smiled, no longer used to the common reduction of the word 'quarter'. 'Indeed,' she said, hastily withdrawing from the quasi-confrontation. 'And may they speak well!'

She thrust a glass of crisp white wine into the midst of the group, where it was met with the clink of a half-dozen others. She scanned the circle in airy fashion as she drank, acutely aware of the unflinching gaze of de Sansa. She soon made her excuses and bowed out of the ring, noticing as she did a slight spinning sensation. How many drinks had she had? It was certainly time to leave.

Annie glided towards the exit, bidding a flurry of farewells as she went. Had she wasted away her magnanimity during that last exchange? Had her discontent been laid bare?

A curse on Rory de Sansa, she thought – and not for the first time in her life.

Ramit was now a mere three minutes away, driving an X-Series Prius. He was a circa four-and-a-half-star Uber recruit. Annie leaned against the wall, feeling as though the role of the winery and her own had been reversed: she the bulging liquor vault, Vinoplex the hollow receptacle. She tracked the progress of Ramit on her phone as he turned off Shoestring Lane and into the final furlong of his approach.

Only when he breezed into view did she detach herself from the wall and turn her attention from screen to scene. She clambered into the back seat of the cab and slumped into a corner.

'Good evening, madam,' came the enthusiastic voice of the driver. 'How are you this evening?' He spoke with a faint Indian accent.

'Delightful, thank you, Ramit,' she responded, forgetting to return the question.

'Fun night, was it?'

'Ups and downs,' she replied. 'Ups and downs.' She could have happily drifted into sleep, but the young taxi driver refused to play ball.

'Well, you must not focus on the downs!' he exclaimed, chuckling to himself. 'What was it, a party?'

'A conference,' she answered, trying to strike a happy balance between brevity and politeness.

'What kind of a conference?'

Annie straightened and stifled a yawn. 'A conference about technology.' She caught the inquisitive gaze of Ramit in the rear-view mirror. 'About using the internet to connect people.' Then there was a pause.

'That sounds very broad!' observed Ramit.

'Yes, well. This afternoon was all about loans.'

'And how are these loans different from any other type of loan?'

'The money…' Annie hesitated. 'In some cases the money comes from ordinary people, like you or me. People who need a bit of extra bang for their buck. They're hooked up to borrowers using the web, and they earn a decent return for lending to them.'

She could barely wrap her swirling head around the old familiar concepts. It was as though her memories were fastened to her by wobbly guy-ropes, and a firm wind could blow them away.

'It's speedier, more flexible finance.' She hiccupped. 'A fairer deal for both sides.' She felt as though she had reeled off an advertisement.

Ramit seemed surprisingly rapt. 'It sounds a bit like Uber,' he said.

'I suppose it does,' said Annie.

'Using the internet to connect people. Fairer. Faster. More flexible. That's the Uber pitch in a nutshell!'

'I suppose it is,' she conceded, making a concerted effort to slow the rotations of the car's interior. She felt the rumbling of canapés from deep within her stomach; caviar-coated crackers were on the move. 'Do you like working for Uber?'

'I don't work *for* Uber,' came the surprisingly swift riposte. 'You work *with* Uber. You build yourself a franchise using it.'

'For a fee, of course.'

'Of course, nothing comes for free in this life, madam! And I'm sorry to say that the fees have been going up lately.'

'Why's that?' asked Annie, genuinely interested but increasingly uncomfortable within the bonds of her seatbelt. The passing blur of London by night had become nauseating.

'In short, because they've won the war!'

'Won?' She stammered. 'War?'

'How many black cabs do you see these days, madam?'

'I…'

'Fewer and fewer, madam!' He answered for her. 'Next to none, in fact. The Uber model has won. More and more drivers are switching over. The more that sign up, the more they can charge.'

'The challenger… Unchallenged,' murmured Annie.

'Exactly, madam!' cried the impassioned and surprisingly keen-eared Ramit. He then slammed on his brakes as a traffic light glared red. Annie lurched forwards in her seat, her stomach slow to follow her. She flailed for the seatbelt and the door handle in unison, rolled out onto the empty pavement and was sick into the gutter. Her embarrassment was mostly swallowed by relief. Instinct had taken over. She didn't know if it was the booze or Ramit's story that her body was rejecting with greater vehemence.

Is there no way to win? she wondered dimly, doubled over and holding a bundle of her hair out of the firing line. What was there to do, when even the usurpers started turning up the heat on the very people they set out to liberate?

Ramit had pulled the car over onto the kerb and was bustling around the bonnet to offer her assistance. Shame now returned after a momentary leave of absence. Ramit made quite a fuss, offering her water and tissues and driving her the remainder of the way home – insisting only that a window remain wide open.

Annie resolved to give him a five-star rating as she slipped into sleep. She suspected he wouldn't return the favour.

2

Secret Victories

They were not far from Mayfair, where the shops are mostly bare.

Elena perched in a shadowy alcove on a poorly lit side road. With her was Sasha, a more recent addition to the outside world, her black skin pimpled by the cold night air. The two women wore matching Puffa jackets, each one lined with a furry hood, each with its sleeves unoccupied. Sasha had chanced a cigarette. She had a packet of gum to hand, but it was still a risk.

'I'm used to the waiting, girl,' said Sasha, as she exhaled a hurried puff. 'But I'll never get used to the cold!'

Elena didn't respond. She wasn't sure that she was used to it either.

Half Moon Street was a good spot for snagging kerb-crawlers. The women's arms were not submerged within their sleeves because they had to be ready to leap to their feet, and couldn't afford to look overdressed; when the headlights of an approaching vehicle came, the coats had to be shrugged off in a hurry. The pair would totter to different bits of the pavement, about halfway and two-thirds of the way along the street. It was each woman for herself, and both knew it. Neither could afford to head home empty-handed.

The car would cruise along the road. The driver would inspect each woman, who in turn would offer him an alluring word or gesture. He would signal his pick with the flick of a wrist, and one of the women would clamber into the vehicle, grateful for the warmth, if little else.

'Won't be long,' Elena assured Sasha.

It had been a long while already. They continued to sit, and to wait, saying little, focusing on retaining bodily warmth. Their rattling breath sent miniature clouds of air into the night.

'Elena,' began Sasha, uncharacteristically tentative in her approach.

'Tell me about that boy from the other night. He didn't look like a client.'

Elena had expected this question. She turned her pretty face to face her friend: slender, framed by pronounced cheekbones, and pale – almost a little pinkish in the cold. As she parted her lips, still not knowing whether she wanted to talk about Mike, a car turned into the street.

The women dropped their coats. Bony joints clicked into action. Sasha half-strode, half-pranced her way towards the spotlight of a lamppost, at once desperate to reach it and damned if she couldn't reach it gracefully. Elena slunk in more reserved fashion to a shadowy spot further along the road.

She didn't begrudge her friend the better spot on this dingy back road. She felt then, as she had felt so many times before, that contorting sensation of being both dogged in doing a thing and loathing the doing of it. Elena would always opt for the second-in-line spot if she could. It was a secret and gratifying form of resistance. Besides, there was no shortage of punters.

Up ahead, Sasha was wheeling around, returning to her perch with a casual swagger. *False alarm*, thought Elena, and she too circled back to the step.

Sasha didn't ask about Mike a second time. Instead the two women sat, quietly content in one another's company. A sad understanding hung between them.

Elena laid her head on Sasha's shoulder, and sung what she could remember of a folksong from her childhood. She had a gentle voice. The strange words – strange now even to her – were caught by the passing gusts of wind and blown away. *Far away*, she hoped. Perhaps far away enough to stand a chance of being answered in a Slavic tongue.

This was not the London of Elena's dreams.

The city had closed in on her from the moment of her arrival. She despised the place. Escaping the claustrophobia of working in the walk-ups had done nothing to help. The people were rude, and often quick to anger – traits that tended to intensify when met with an accented protest. She had dreamed of a city of gentle people, and wide cobbled streets. She had found a whole country full of balding, shabby men who spat into the gutters and squinted at passing girls. *Ah, could this be one now?*

Light once again pierced the darkness, and the women took their places on the pavement. The vehicle was difficult to make out. Dark, brown perhaps, box-like, angular. There was an oversized grille placed a little skewiff between the headlights. As it rolled towards Sasha, its flaking paintwork became apparent. The chassis was beaten up too, and one of the two observable hubcaps had been patched over with gaffer tape.

The vehicle – an ageing make of Rover – had slowed alongside Sasha. It almost stopped entirely. But the lure of what lay beyond had clearly won over the driver. The battered wheels rolled on, leaving Sasha to wrap up her act with whatever dignity she could muster.

Elena continued to survey the approaching car. The wipers must be broken; build-ups of dust and muck clung to the windscreen. The vehicle had a tinted sunroof, which looked as though it had been added as an afterthought, perhaps following a mistake on the part of the manufacturer. Elena absorbed herself with the idea that this trundling mess was nothing more than an accidental soft-top, and that at any moment the whole thing might collapse upon itself. Anything, after all, to avoid thinking about its contents.

Slowly, the left-hand window began to recede into the door frame. The vision of a man loomed into view. One set of his stubby fingers grasped the wheel, the other was laid on the gearstick. He wore a beige zip-up jacket. His face was milky and puffed, and he had the hair of a man who should have resigned himself to baldness long ago. His gaze was a mixture of sheepishness and desire.

The rickety old Rover was going so slowly that its eventual halt was now inevitable. Elena was ready to begin the process of walling herself off, which involved a mental retreat far into herself. But there first remained some work to be done, in this perverse form of fishing.

Fishing was how she had been told to think of it. Here was a fat, silvery trout, wriggling half-heartedly, only too eager to be hooked. She played the fisherwoman – bound to the hunt, loathe to reel in her prize. She pressed her upper arms into her sides and bent at the waist, lowering her head to window height. She delayed lifting her forehead for a half-moment, expertly connecting eyes with her adversary when she did. He was won, a rank and sorry prize. He raised a fleshy paw and beckoned her inside with a jerk of the fingers. She accepted, clambering numbly into the vehicle, which smelled no fresher than it looked. Her mind was ready to bolt, but she could not afford to shut down yet. Negotiations were pending.

'Good evening,' wheezed the jittery client.

'Hey there, sweetheart. How may I be of service?'

Sweetheart was what to call them. But Elena had chosen the other words carefully, wishing to establish from the outset that this was a place of business. Too often men duped themselves into believing that these things were driven by mutual desire. The thought of it made Elena want to be sick. She would abide by the rules, but there would be no feigned sense of enjoyment. And if that made her less desirable, so be it. These were the micro-sized struggles that kept her mind balanced. And, again, there was no shortage of punters.

With a whimper, the man elucidated his desires. He drove as they entered into conference. The car croaked and rocked. He would only hint at what he wanted, as he hadn't the nerve to say it plainly. Elena had to tease it out of him, which she despised.

'It'll be fifty pounds,' she announced flatly. The man frowned, his chubby face reddening and contorting.

'That's more than I've paid elsewhere,' he blurted, unwittingly revealing the routine nature of the night's digression.

'That is the price,' replied Elena.

He hadn't the backbone to argue. He was the kind of weak-willed customer who regularly swears off the habit. He was cognisant of market value, but acutely aware of the shamefulness of the act, and so easily disarmed in negotiations. Eventually he conceded, as if it were a mercy to the girl. Elena wore only the thinnest pretence of allure. She would ensure that he knew this charade for what it was.

The car clunked slowly to a halt in some godforsaken dead end, partially obscured from the outside world by a half-open skip. Elena faded. She tied back her hair, barely aware of the blood in her fingertips. The man awkwardly unbuckled himself, spilling out over his belt. Wheezing, he lowered his trousers and his chequered, moth-eaten boxer shorts. His penis stood upright and ragged.

So it began. It was simply a matter of attachment and detachment, a primitive coaxing of the flesh. The motion was mechanical, and if the lack of variety displeased him, then Elena was glad. It was another secret victory. Her mind wandered as her body endured.

She thought of home, of shabby houses in ramshackle roads, of the stews and their spices, of the local lads. Hardship was no stranger to those streets, but it came and it went. Here there was no respite. Her mind was weaving its way back towards the moment.

She diverted its course, swerving now for Mike, and the memory of the night they had shared together in Soho a week ago. She had felt so free that evening. They had, at Mike's recommendation, taken part as volunteers in an immersive theatre production – serving together as members of a counterfeit crowd. The production itself was structured as a sort of ride. 'Passengers' – as they were referred to – were flung from one surreal scene to the next, oblivious as to what each twist and turn would bring.

Passenger after passenger had floated by them and away that night. Fair-weather escapists, one and all – committed only to an hour or more of light-hearted uncertainty.

A pudgy hand had been laid upon the back of Elena's neck, snapping her back to reality. She jerked her head backwards.

'Get off,' she said instinctively.

If they pay, they play. The words had been drilled into her, but she couldn't help herself. Fortunately, he didn't protest. But from then on, Elena struggled to lose herself, and was forced to endure the transaction untempered. The man's sniffs and grunts filled her with nausea.

At last it was over. Elena opened the car door and spat forcefully into the night air. She straightened herself, hair dishevelled. The man was already busily repositioning his clothes.

'Fifty,' he said, through heavy breaths, counting out a wad of greasy notes. He handed her the stack and smiled.

'Thank you.' The words stung. She didn't bother to count the money.

As she made to leave, the man spoke again. 'I'm sorry,' he began. 'I…'

He faltered. Elena gave him no time to recover.

'Thank you,' she repeated, pulling on her puffer coat and scampering away from the rusty car.

3

Go

'Clock's ticking, Veronica,' said Annie.

The board was playing out in Veronica's favour, as often it tended to. Café Craft was bustling around them. There were the usual sounds of the baristas twisting levers and frothing up milk, and of metal beakers being banged on thick wooden counters.

'I fear the corner is lost, old girl,' said Veronica. She laid a saucer-shaped black tile on the board, sealing off a number of white tiles. She then leaned back into her cushioned wooden chair and took a sip of coffee with a satisfied expression. Annie's empty matcha latte cup lay idle on the table.

'Perhaps. But not the war.'

Annie watched the board intently, brow furrowed, her tangled mane made static by thought. She was outmatched by Veronica, who could see further ahead and play out conflict scenarios across the board in computer-like fashion. Rarely would she lay a tile before the full three minutes' worth of sand had slipped into the lower chamber. Annie, on the other hand, was hastier – in part, she reasoned, so as not to give Veronica quite so long to run her calculations.

'So, to return to the DisTech event,' said Veronica.

'Must we?'

'You're pleased to have gone?' Veronica persisted.

Annie laid her next tile close to the black wall that encircled her allies in the northwest region of the board.

'I found the whole thing cathartic, since you ask,' she said. 'I feel as though I can move on. I think that may have been why I was sick, come to think of it.' A glint flickered in her eye. She knew exactly how to rile Veronica.

'The champagne may also have been a factor,' said Veronica coolly.

Annie was well aware of her friend's edge in *Go*, but she knew too that Veronica didn't take her lightly. Annie never entered into an encounter without a tactical twist or two up her sleeve. They didn't always pan out, of course, but grand designs were at play – that much was certain. Veronica tended to focus on the games within the game, the skirmishes that inevitably sprang up around the board as space diminished. While Annie schemed, Veronica's tactic was to sweep the building blocks from beneath her.

'I'm glad, Annie. Truly.'

'Mind on the prize, Ron,' replied Annie, to which Veronica returned a knowing smile. She then set about assailing another of her friend's trembling outposts.

'And when was your last meeting?'

'Meeting?' replied Annie absentmindedly.

'Yes, meeting,' repeated Veronica. 'When was your last AA meeting?'

'Oh those!' exclaimed Annie. 'God, I haven't been to one of those in yonks, and am much better for it.'

There was a pause.

'I'm concerned about what happened, Annie.'

'Oh, Veronica!' said Annie. 'Don't fuss. Yes, I had too much to drink. That can happen to anyone. Don't make it more than that. Don't look for meaning where there ain't none.'

Veronica returned her barely diminished coffee to its resting place and once again entered into meditation. 'Well, if you're sure,' she said, after a while.

'Trust me,' said Annie.

'OK.'

The game dragged on. Veronica's mind was trained, split between only the coffee and the board. Annie's mind was everywhere. She consulted her phone regularly. She glanced up as new faces filed into the café. She whipped through a nearby paper a few pages at a time, occasionally stopping to remark on a headline.

One item above all others piqued her attention. She leaned in further over the two-page spread, as if to dive in head first, and for a few turns appeared to throw down her tiles with no regard whatsoever for strategy.

'Appalling!' she declared, her Irish blood coursing. 'Absolutely appalling.' She stole a glance up at Veronica, who continued to be absorbed by the board. She twisted the story around for Veronica – whose eyes seemed frozen still behind her rimless, rectangular spectacles.

'Veronica,' she persisted, 'have you seen this?'

'If you're trying to distract me, Annie, it isn't going to work.'

'Women are being slain in the streets, Veronica! Never you mind your fallen tiles.'

Veronica raised an eyebrow. All of her tiles were in play, and quite well. But it was clear that the game would progress no further while the newspaper lay untended. Reluctantly, she stilled the slipping sand grains, laying down the timer horizontally.

The story, which orbited in chunks around a photo of a wailing woman, was entitled, 'Exposing the violent world of prostitution in London.' Various tables and statistics were dotted around the central image – a galaxy of suffering, spinning upon the tabletop.

The numbers painted a picture of a rising tide of violence towards London's burgeoning community of prostitutes. An estimated 152 sex workers had been murdered between 1990 and 2015, with such incidents growing in frequency. The perpetrators of these acts, at a glance, were 'shadowy' pimps and 'wretched' punters, with the former bearing the greater part of the columnist's ire. The words 'There were 1,139 victims of trafficking for sexual exploitation in 2014' were blown up in large font.

The report lambasted government and law enforcement officials for their apparent unwillingness to intervene. It suggested that the current laws on brothel-keeping had forestalled women from working together, thus exposing them to the obvious risks of working alone. But more damaging, in the mind of the columnist at least, was the fact that it remained illegal to solicit for sex – in spite of recent recommendations to the contrary. The law on soliciting was said to prevent sex workers from seeking help to break free of prostitution, while also exposing them to the risk of abuse.

Veronica scanned the spread for a couple of minutes before looking up blankly at Annie, apparently none the wiser as to why she had been made to read it. Annie was watching her expectantly, intensely.

Veronica looked uneasy, as if aware that something had stirred beneath her friend's scattered hash of hair. 'Quite shocking,' she said.

'*Quite* shocking?'

Veronica's face fell. This wasn't the first time her friend had pulled her up for 'emotional detachment'. Annie would often say that Veronica thought too hard about how to express her feelings; things didn't come as naturally to her as they did to Annie. Nor did they come as hotly.

'You find the abuse and battery of your fellow woman *quite* shocking?'

'I didn't mean that,' replied Veronica. 'It's bad. Very bad.'

'Very bad indeed,' snapped Annie, her chin jutting. 'How can nobody be stepping in?'

'Well. The victims here are also criminals, of a kind.'

Annie's eyebrows were close to escaping her brow altogether.

'Technically,' added Veronica.

'To a far lesser degree, and for no fault of their own, I'd wager.'

'Still,' said Veronica, warily. 'Small surprise that the underworld is being left to its own devices.'

'Like delegating hell to the devil,' said Annie, irked at the apparent indifference of her friend.

'Exactly.'

'That's no system at all.' Annie continued to look at her intently.

'Agreed,' offered Veronica.

She reached for the sand timer, but Annie wasn't finished.

'I've spent four years getting myself balanced, Ron,' said Annie, toying with a packet of brown sugar. Her tone had clearly shifted. 'You've been wonderful to me in that time. And I know that I've often failed to repay the favour.'

'Annie...' began Veronica.

'I'm starting something.'

Veronica's visible discomfort now morphed into fully fledged concern. Perhaps sensing a backlash of sorts, Annie continued.

'Years of idleness, of counselling, of concentrated quiet. What was the point of it all if not to get me back to the point where I can do something worthwhile with my life?'

Veronica looked deeply into Annie's eyes. The women were quite different. Veronica was a vision of calm and order; her hair fell naturally into black, creaseless curtains. Her clothes were worn deliberately, for function over flair, but with a sensible colour scheme all the same. She wore no jewellery of any kind, and she had no piercings. Annie was erratic, bold, imperfect and energised.

'Do you not worry that the stress will be too much?' said Veronica, with enormous care.

'You don't even know what I'm doing yet!' said Annie, half-joking. 'I worry more about the prospect of an aimless existence.'

This line came off as somewhat rehearsed, as indeed it had been. A long pause ensued. The space between the two friends felt suddenly stretched, as though their armchairs were flying away in opposite directions – off into uncharted territories. For nearly three years, their weekly visits to the corner-street café had been skipped only a handful of times. They had shared many coffees, and many a game of *Go*.

'What I mean is, are you certain you want to burden yourself with whatever this venture is?' asked Veronica, eventually.

'I am.'

Veronica slouched backwards, uncharacteristically. Once decided upon a course of action, Annie was notoriously difficult to redirect. 'Well then. What is this plan?' she enquired.

Annie reached out an unclasped hand and laid her fingers upon the open newspaper. Her bony knuckles whitened, as if she was straining to tattoo the text onto her friend's brain. Veronica looked down again at the paper. Her eyes flitted from the pained expression of the pictured woman, to the author's name, to the boxed quote in the upper regions of the second page.

Annie watched as Veronica spotted it: the date was off. The paper was several weeks old. She had feared her friend would cotton on sooner. But now it was too late; the ambush was set. As Veronica rose up in protest, Annie interjected.

'Here,' began Annie, pointedly, 'is an extreme, but familiar cycle.

Familiar for us, at least. Here, Ron, is an ecosystem that is as dysfunctional, violent, and as plagued by inefficiency and opacity as any on the planet.'

Veronica listened – begrudgingly, but intently.

'The more powerful the middleman, the more difficult he is to unseat. You've said it to me many times. Veronica, you just said it yourself, these pimps run the back-alleys unopposed.' Annie spoke with a fiery intensity. 'For centuries they've sat between punter and prostitute, filling their boots in exchange for what, in reality, amounts to little more than an introduction. They're often arbitrarily cruel. They're usually violent. And they are all of them outdated.' Silent energy fizzed between the two women. 'Their run is at an end, Ron. We can end it.'

'No.' The answer fell from Veronica's mouth with a thud at the mention of *we*. 'Annie…' she paused, eyes casting around as if searching for somebody to corroborate the ridiculousness of the discussion. 'This is not a game of beat the bank. It's a game of life or death. The players are violent. The field is full of shadows. I see already what you're proposing, and it can't work.'

'Ah!' cried Annie, slapping two hands together triumphantly. 'Then your mind has already leaped to the same conclusion as mine. A network…'

'No,' repeated Veronica.

'A marketplace…'

'No. It will not work. It can't. The people you are proposing to help are not middle-class families with some spare cash. They're criminals, Annie.'

'Do you really believe that?' flared Annie. 'Criminals? No sane woman enters into the sex trade of her own volition. They come tumbling in through the worst assortment of routes imaginable. Trafficking, destitution, addiction. These are criminals?'

'So your solution,' came Veronica's swift reply, 'is to take the whole dirty business online? Yes?'

'Yes,' said Annie. Her right hand had not left the paper, but now it was pressed flat against the table.

'An Uber for the sex trade, right? Annie…' Veronica shook her head in reply to the fervent nods of her friend. 'The streamlining of prostitution? Can't you hear the silliness of it? What would it solve?'

One corner of Annie's lips flicked upwards, almost imperceptibly. She marvelled at her friend's capacity for reading her. She smiled inwardly at what she knew to be flashing through Veronica's mind. It was like looking into a mirror that returned a slightly crooked version of the self.

'You have to accept that a bad thing – even an awful thing – is happening before you can hope to fix it,' said Annie. 'Prostitution happens. It always has. Perhaps it always will. We can at least strive to ensure that it happens in an equitable way. We can give women who've plunged themselves into the practice of selling their bodies a fighting chance of escape. That is what I believe, Ron. I'm from the school of harm reduction. Clean needles for drug addicts, and all that.'

Veronica fidgeted, wincing at each fresh mention of the word *we*. She was captured in a landslide, borne towards an inevitable conclusion.

'Annie,' she began wearily. 'I will not be swayed this time. I am sorry. Truly.' Neither of them said anything for a moment. 'But give me the plan, in full, if only so that I can better advise you against it.'

For the rest of that sunny afternoon in Fulham, Veronica listened to her friend. Annie pitched feverishly; she was well practised at it. Veronica objected intermittently.

They didn't return to their board game for some hours. When they finally did, it took five moves for Veronica to realise her undoing. Annie's seemingly defeated clusters suddenly began to coalesce. Veronica fought to sever connections where she could, but her friend soon commanded a wall that covered two-thirds of the board. At the softening of the early evening sun, and without having lost a single saucer-shaped tile, Veronica conceded defeat.

4

Sacrifice

It was late. The drone of passing traffic had begun to splutter outside. The rest of the office had darkened, alive only in the form of the dim, greenish bars of light that illuminated the fire exits.

Warren sat quite still at his desk. He occupied a glass-walled cubicle in the corner of the station. Before him were neatly stacked piles of paperwork, zip lock bags, mustard-coloured folders, a laptop and a mug full of pens and pencils.

The spacing between objects was pleasingly regular. A filing cabinet stood against the wall with its drawers labelled. A furry, pin-stricken board rose up behind him. A dark coat hung precisely on its peg. An empty bin sat in the corner. A printer full of paper was humming, duetting with the pervasive buzz of the building. There was a cupboard in the corner. There was bourbon and a glass.

Warren married the two together, filling the tumbler a third full. He watched the amber liquid slip between and buoy the melting ice, then let the contents settle into a slowly spinning face-off. There could only be one winner. His gaze was absent. His mind was elsewhere.

In the cupboard rested piles of paper – pages and pages of cases closed, and meticulously filed. There were menial misdemeanours, unspeakable acts, riddles, clues and facts. The shelves sagged with the weight of information. A row of crisp white shirts hung from a suspended pole, a supply which Warren replenished on each and every Monday morning, so that he might run to work for the remainder of the week. This being a Tuesday, three remained. Behind the shirts, propped up at an angle against the cupboard frame, was a board. It was perhaps the one thing in the office that appeared out of place. Its spongy corkwood behind was turned towards the doors.

Warren didn't need to retrieve the board to consider its display. It bore a lattice of connections and coincidences and crime, one that he could easily visualise. He often wondered why he had kept the damned thing at all. Perhaps it was because Superintendent Payne knew that he still had it. More often he wondered why he so often found himself contemplating it, fretting over it, running restless thoughts along its tender linkages.

It really was late. Laura would worry. The girls would be sound asleep. He should go. In truth, he didn't know why he had stayed this long, but for months now Warren had found himself, night after night, anchored to his desk until late, fingering the lid of a whiskey bottle.

The work on the desk was long since finished. Multiple incidences of domestic abuse lurked within the pages, mostly involving male violence towards female partners, and the suspicions of neighbours, or social workers, or do-gooders of some other variety.

Warren had found grounds to take action on each of them. That action involved meetings, surveillance, questioning; it rarely amounted to intervention. Such attempts were most often met with confusion, or indignation, or rage, for often the victims were so impossibly entangled within the net of affection and affliction that they had become inseparable from its barbs, believing that the pain of extraction would outweigh the pain of staying put. The suggestion that one person could hurt the other was absurd, or excusable, understandable, or hidden away.

Warren glanced at his digital watch. 22:06. He really must head home. However, he distrusted the number six and had done for many years, and would at least stay put until the minute ticked by. He drained the glass of whiskey and leaned deep into his chair, which itself leaned backwards a little towards the wall. He felt weariness in his limbs and in his neck as he rolled his head back to face the ceiling. A tiredness clung to him that would not be assuaged by sleep. It was a tiredness of the heart. He felt lessened, slighter, every time he filed away a paper pile of the kind that now festered on his desk. Like the ice that was lazily disintegrating into liquid, he could feel himself dissolving.

Once more his mind returned to the board. He surveyed it. It throbbed in the cupboard like some hellish organ. Every scattered pin and scribbled note and photograph was etched onto his brain. One photograph above all filled him with a heavy, hopeless anger. The man in the image wore a slim-fitted suit jacket and shirt. His eyes were dark and deeply set. His dark hair was slicked backwards and he wore a thick, carefully kempt beard. His name was Emerson Smith, and many a taut cotton string had been pinned to the perimeter of his image.

He was not alone in the central region of the board. He was in the dark company of Bledi Shala, Reed McCoy and Emilio Marques. But Smith was the worst of them. He was not the most oppressive, and certainly was not the most violent, but his was a quiet, cancerous kind of evil. His grip was the tightest – a hegemony that many of the women whose lives and every action he controlled mistook for care, or even for love.

Warren thought of the board as layers of bedrock. Most of the pimps were vicious and volatile, but had only fleeting careers. They were almost interchangeable. They were terrifying, but largely unoriginal and uncontrolled. Some possessed more staying power than others, of course, but most were eroded by the passing of time. Smith was the base layer – an impenetrable slate, lying always beneath the buffer of lesser matter.

Warren realised that he was standing, facing the cupboard. It was now 22:21. He then resolved to embark upon the long and arduous journey that would culminate in him leaving the station. Reaching that point was no simple task. The switches had to be tended to first, and often they were tended to twice, for he was rarely able to assure himself that he had seen to them satisfactorily the first time. All of the blinds had to be drawn. Every one of the doors had to be closed until they clicked shut. Then they had to be double-checked.

When it came to the desktops, Warren had to straighten scattered objects, but in such a way that the interference would go unnoticed. The particularly messy desks he left alone, for they were moulded to their natural milieu. To the more sparsely littered desks, he tended only lightly. He set what bits of stationery there were parallel to one another, as one might arrange a pair of shoes. If any object was balanced over the edge of a surface, like frozen water over a fall, he would reposition it so that it was once more rooted to the desk.

Warren also felt a compulsion to inspect parts of the office that might otherwise go uninspected for months or even years on end. This was partially because he pitied them their isolation. He thus included in his nightly routine a cursory visual sweep of the dusty tops of the filing cabinets that stood in a long line against one wall. He had to stand on a chair to do this, but it only took him a moment.

As a young teenager, Warren had once discovered a mouse drowned in the depths of a school toilet in the early hours of the morning. It had occurred to him then that simply closing the toilet lid overnight would have spared the mouse its life. He had therefore made it his business to close every lid in the gents before leaving the station each night.

These were but a few of the duties he performed on a nightly basis, but they give a flavour of his sacrifice, which is certainly how Warren saw it. For it felt as though to not do all of these things would invite some unutterable doom down upon him, or upon his loved ones, and while he knew that to be absurd, he found still greater absurdity in running such risk for the sake of twenty or thirty minutes of madness each night.

Finally, the burly detective pulled his high-collared duffle coat close and made for the exit, breaking out into the cool night air. He felt freer of mind the further he got from the station, but never completely released. He was relieved only by a chiding from his wife, who had indeed been worrying for some time.

5

The Incumbent

Elena gazed defiantly into the face of the large leather-jacketed doorman. Sasha had drifted from her vision, escaping around the corner. Benz wore a dark beanie hat, pulled down to his eyebrows. He grinned menacingly, his oddly dotted golden teeth glinting in the low street light.

'You're expected,' he said.

Elena wasn't scared, not of Benz. She'd dealt with him and his kind more than enough times, on more than enough nights. No, she wasn't scared of Benz.

'Well, you gonna let me up?' she said.

Benz's stupid grin snapped shut. His pupils bulged. His head twitched. But then his better sense prevailed, and he stepped aside.

Elena had never spent more than a few fleeting seconds with Emerson Smith, but she had heard the stories. Years before she had worked in his brothels and his walk-ups. Among her clients were politicians, businessmen and bored and wealthy husbands. Men who somehow allowed themselves to lose touch with the ugliness of their twilight pastimes, or who fooled themselves into believing that they were bound to their purchases by genuine affection. They treated Elena as well as could be expected, most of the time, but the terms stated clearly enough that nothing was off-limits. *If they pay, they play.*

But those strange, narrow townhouses were long behind her. Several years ago she had been tossed out into the night to work the London streets alongside Sasha and a fleet of similarly miserable women. The right to work beyond the bounds of confinement was seen as a privilege. Mr Smith trusted her; his trust was not to be betrayed.

The stairwell ahead was surprisingly shabby. A diamond-patterned carpet took her high-heeled feet upwards. It had frayed at the borders and was worn in the middle. The light was low, the dull offering of a few naked light bulbs. The air wore a certain dankness, as though the whole structure had been recently exhumed from deep within a watery grave, and left to drip itself dry.

Elena felt uneasy, out of place. She reached the summit of the staircase. Without taking the time to properly compose herself, she knocked on the door.

'Come in.'

It was a cockney, measured voice, perilously comforting. Like the stairway, the room was an odd mixture of décor and dilapidation, and must surely have belonged to the same sunken ship from which the staircase had been salvaged. Polished, ceiling-high cabinets housed row upon row of dusty old books. A matching, heavily burdened desk sat before the cabinets, and between the two was Emerson Smith.

His body was bent double over a ledger of some kind, his mind seemingly elsewhere. He wore a slim-fitted black shirt and had a great tangled beard on his chin and cheeks. He didn't look up.

'Sit,' he said.

Elena obeyed, her heart raging. She perched herself upon the chair opposite him, unsure how to position her body, which felt suddenly jumpy and unfamiliar.

Then his eyes were on her. 'May I share a passage with you, Elena?'

She didn't know what to say. 'Yes,' she eventually whispered. 'Yes, of course, Mr Smith.'

He continued to absorb her for a moment longer. Truly, it felt to Elena as though she was ebbing away. But now he was standing, retrieving a small book from the cabinet side. A Bible, it seemed, with page corners crumpled throughout. His finger and thumb separated the scripture and he held it up.

'He who withholds his rod hates his son, but he who loves him disciplines him diligently. What do you make of that, Elena?'

'I don't know,' she blurted, trying not to engage in what she guessed was a game of cat and mouse.

'Tell me what you think it means.'

'It's about raising kids, right?' She raised her eyes to meet his.

'That's right!' He clapped, maniacally, wheeling back around to the safer side of his desk. The suddenness of his movements alarmed her. 'That's exactly right.'

He reoccupied his seat, reclining deep into the green leather padding, and surveyed Elena once more. He spent a long while there, seemingly enjoying her discomfort.

'You know, I don't buy into any of that shit. I don't believe in heaven or hell. I don't believe in the judgement of God. Ah!' Suddenly his posture sharpened, and he wagged a finger at her. 'But I do believe in judgement.' He laughed.

'Mr Smith,' began Elena, judging the aftermath of a laugh, however sinister, as the best time for her to cut in. She was scared to anger him, but she was also afraid of allowing his performance to roll on uninterrupted. He seemed like the dramatic sort. 'Why have you called me in here, boss? Have I done something wrong?'

His left eye twitched. She looked down; in her experience, down was the safest way to look.

'This,' he said, twisting the ledger in front of him to face Elena, 'is my business. You'll find records for every working girl that I manage in London within these pages. Once a day, in the evening, I balance the book. I have myself a drink. I go to sleep happy.'

Elena sat stone still, her eyes flitting across the open page of the bloated ledger.

'Would you please turn to "S"?'

S for Stoyan, she assumed. Elena Stoyan. She fingered the letter and peeled the preceding pages back. Emerson now stood by her side. He watched her closely; she dared not look up. Elena flicked through the pages of her life, through all her many labours. She reached the Saturday, yesterday, when she had last turned a trick. It was a £100 job. It was there, immortalised in ink. Elena felt a flutter of relief. She jerked her face up to his.

'Up to date, boss.' It was half statement, half query.

Smith straightened. His hands found his pockets. His bushy eyebrows climbed his forehead and he ran his fingers through his hair. He turned and wandered to the window, where moonlight seeped reluctantly through the shutters. He placed a leather boot on the sill.

'How are you, socially?'

The inquiry caught Elena off guard.

'Good.' She spoke cautiously.

'Are you taking well to London?'

'I have been living here for years.' For fear her remark seemed chiding, she went on: 'I still struggle with the cold.'

'And how is your sex life?'

Elena froze. 'Lucrative,' she answered.

Emerson roared with laughter once more. 'Come now, Elena,' he said, marching over to the desk and taking a seat on the edge closest to her. 'There are no secrets between family.'

He reached out his hands and took hers in a loose grip. The connection was abhorrent. Elena felt as though she was being tried on, like an item of clothing, that he was wriggling his self into her. She was defenceless.

His grip tightened. 'Tell me more about this Mike?'

Mike. How could that name have found its way into this place? It was as if the most thinly filmed bubble had fluttered between them, skin shimmering stubbornly through the pulverising dark of the abyss. She had to protect it.

'It is Mike, isn't it?' he asked.

'Just a boy. He's just a boy that I've been seeing a bit.'

'A bit more than a bit, from what I hear,' said Emerson. There was menace in his voice. He reached for the tumultuous ledger. 'Shall I enter him in?'

'It's not like that.' Elena's mind flapped. How much did he know?

'Are you sleeping together?'

'A few times.' She paused. 'Just a few times. But not in the way that you think. He doesn't pay.'

'Everybody pays, Elena!' he roared, snapping the open ledger shut.

After a time, he stood, returning his hands to his pockets, then withdrawing them again. Elena couldn't look at him. It was all she could do to keep control, experienced in self-stifling though she was.

'Look at me,' he demanded.

Elena obeyed.

'Your mistake, Elena, is believing that this arm, for example, is your arm. That these hairs on your head are your hairs. That your body is yours to do with as you please. It is not. You are to be deployed as I – and I alone – see fit. Do you understand?'

She nodded, though her heart was filled with rage. She began to lower her head, but Smith caught her by the chin.

'As to your actions,' he said, 'should I withhold judgement?' His wild eyes hunted hers. His wiry beard was millimetres from her chin. 'Should I not use the rod?'

Only later that night did Elena realise what he meant – that he was harking back to his earlier biblical bluster. He held her in a vice, scanning her, weighing her, consuming her. Elena strained to appear deferent, to stop her rage from bursting through.

Then he recoiled. 'No,' he said. 'Better left unspoiled. Go.'

Cautiously, Elena rose from the chair. She offered a quirky curtsy and made for the door, her limbs not yet fully returned to her.

'Elena,' Emerson called after her, as she neared the doorway. 'Never see that man again. I've been good to you. I trusted you to work the streets. Never see him again, Elena. For his sake, and yours.'

'I won't, boss.'

He nodded. And with that, Elena hauled open the door, and escaped.

Her descent of the stairs was a frantic paddle to the light. She broke into the night air, levered her body free. She was past Benz in a flash. Her feet carried her around a corner, and deep into an alleyway. She squatted, clawing at her hair, her painted cheeks. She screamed a silent scream. It was the only kind she knew.

6

Beta Testing

Annie lingered on a street corner in Southwark. It was early in the evening, barely five o'clock, but night had long since laid itself upon the city. She was propped against a stylish lamppost, the kind that wound itself up in knots towards the top.

Around her the roads and pavements bustled. Men in suits and lengthy overcoats strode this way and that. Children in uniform were being hurried along by their mothers, who struggled under the weight of two or more school bags. Elderly men grimaced as they shuffled by, absorbing everything with an air of suspicion – Annie included.

Close by, a grubby man was slumped against the wall of an apartment block, his legs hidden beneath a grubbier sleeping bag. A small Costa coffee cup stood beside him, cradling no more than seventy pence. Annie wondered how regularly he emptied its contents. There would, of course, be an optimal amount. It wouldn't do for it to appear too full, nor for it to be entirely empty. Strange, she thought, how even beggars must demonstrate a track record of success – as if a few pennies in the cup confer a kind of perverse legitimacy on their plight.

She felt for the phone in her pocket. She unlocked it and swiped in search of the latest addition to her vast collection of apps. There it was. The endeavour on which she was now embarked. Pimple.

The word was written in a sleek white font beneath a red square, which was branded with a similarly snaking capital *P*, also in white. The project appeared to have arrived at Annie, rather than the other way around. She had been gazing in awe at a distinct but far-off cloud from the confines of a creeping funicular. Suddenly she was within.

Annie's eureka moment had not, in fact, been quite as original as she had first imagined. A similar concept – albeit one constrained by the technology of its day – had already risen and fallen in San Francisco.

It had been called RedBook and it began in the Bay Area in 1999 as an online discussion forum for punters. The site soon morphed into an organ for advertisement, match making, rating and many more of the processes demanded by the sex trade. It offered women a measure of safety, in so much as they were able, to a certain extent, to vet their customers. It also offered discretion, pulling women off the streets and into the shadowy confines of the World Wide Web.

RedBook had been the beating heart of West Coast prostitution right up until early 2014, when its founder Eric 'Red' Omuro was arrested on various charges, including racketeering and money laundering – but not before having pulled in over $5 million in profits.

The machinery had lacked a certain level of sophistication, hence Mr Omuro's undoing. But the site had also lacked what Annie described as 'Uberisation'. The lewd advertisements were static and the matchmakings were not facilitated in a timely fashion. RedBook could not bring together two souls at the very point of need. But Pimple could.

Annie pressed her thumb to the ambient *P* and entered into the world of Pimple – of which she was the architect in chief. It was still a little rough around the edges, and navigationally clunky, but the core functionalities were in place. Annie was already signed in as one of only two existing users. The screen morphed into a map at the touch of her thumb. At the epicentre was a small icon, shaped like a sexless person, over which hovered a solitary *AO*.

Annie O'Mahony was alone in the ether, for now. Hidden stage right of the screen was a crudely composed menu – offering her the ability to tinker with various facets of the app. A *Settings* optionality could be used to update payment details, fiddle with price points, extend the technology's geographical reach in the style of the dating app Tinder and so on. The *Profile* section afforded users the chance to curate the superficial side of the app. Pimple profiles could be adorned with everything from pictures to short biographies, even through to video content. Annie's profile had already been heavily decorated. *Alerts*, *Messages* and *History* tabs had also been installed, their efficaciousness now set to be tested.

Annie waited. She toyed with the little red icon, picking her up and setting her down on a nearby street before returning her to the street corner where the real-life Annie loitered.

A sudden bottleneck of passers-by forced her to take a step closer to the nearby wall, and then to flatten herself against it. Grumbles sounded. The pavement ran thick with vexation. Eyes narrowed. Shoulders hunched. *AO*, on the other hand, had the whole of a virgin digital plane in which to wander.

Suddenly, the mobile device vibrated – a sharp and solitary throb. *VC has requested the pleasure of your company.* Annie read the message. A note of satisfaction fluttered in her chest. *Accept?* Or *Decline?* She thumbed her way to acquiescence. *Your client will arrive in six minutes.* So far, so good.

Buzz. *New message.* The mysterious *VC* comes a-calling.

Test, read the message.

Hey honey, you look gorgeous :) replied Annie. Veronica often spoke of her loathing for so-called emoticons, describing them as a gross perversion of grammatical apparatus.

How can you tell? returned the still unfleshed account of *VC*. But no reply was forthcoming, for the borders of *AO*'s solitary plane of existence had just been breached. *VC* was in range. Annie's attention now switched to monitoring the progress of the second human icon as it inched across the little screen. It was just a few streets away. As the icon drew nearer, so too did the minutes fall away from the *Time till arrival* meter, and a nervous excitement built within Annie's belly.

Somehow none of this Pimple business had felt especially likely to happen until now. Veronica had committed to building the thing, and to contemplating it, and to discussing it, in what she said was merely an exercise in humouring a dear friend. It would never come to anything. But now that the first of the network's ties had been forged, Pimple had taken on a sudden and embryonic vivacity.

VC seemed to be hurtling towards *AO*, eating up the pixels at a rate of perhaps half a millimetre a second. Soon the vehicle loomed into worldly view. Its make, model and number plate were attached to *VC*'s initial gambit, making her clearly identifiable. It would not do, after all, for punters and prostitutes to spend time fumbling around the streets for one another. Discretion was the name of the game. The red Mazda RX8 – number plate LF52 7RR – pulled up alongside Annie. The window of the driver's seat wound down, and there was Veronica Cheung.

'Hey doll,' Annie cooed.

'Climb on in,' said Veronica.

Annie had already circumnavigated the stern of the vehicle and was clambering into the passenger seat. She was in a rambunctious mood.

'Give me a kiss, baby,' she said, leaning in towards her friend.

'So I'd say the matchmaking functionality is working pretty smoothly,' said Veronica, as Annie retreated in mock deflation. 'Shall we test the transaction process?'

'I do so love it when you talk dirty,' said Annie.

Veronica barely stifled a smile. 'Annie,' she snapped, doing her best to sound stern. 'If we are to be serious about this, then let us be serious.'

'Oh, you old bore!' Annie laughed, shaking her curls. 'OK, OK. Right you are. Pull up over there.' They had driven on, and now pulled in to the car park of a small petrol station.

'I have confirmed via the app that we're together,' began Veronica. This could only be done by vendors. 'You should now be able to select from a range of options, with price points attached. Do you see?'

'I do. Here we are. Right then, let me see. Let me see.'

Annie feigned a painful decision-making process by chewing on the insides of her cheeks, before settling on the option of *Fourth Base*. In the name of discretion, punters would not simply select a carnal act. Instead, they would adhere to a near-enough universal code. The options on offer included *First Base*, *Second Base*, *Third Base* and *Fourth Base*. It would be for the punters and their quarries to discern the meaning of each term. Each option carried its own cost, and a number of options could be packaged up together. Women were even able to offer combination deals as incentives.

Prior to submitting her own selection, Annie decided to barter a little. The price for *Fourth Base* – sexual intercourse – with *VC* ranged from £250 to £300. Ordinary sex workers in London saw around twenty-five clients a week, paying an average rate of £78 per visit. The two women had decided to enable bartering to reflect the simple fact that not all punters are born equal, with some bound to be deemed far fouler than others. Annie logged an offer of £260.

'Think I'm cute enough to get away with that?'

'I'll allow it,' replied Veronica, with a little grin. She accepted the proposal, and the two women let some time pass. They talked of the feel of either side of the Pimple app: how seamlessly their linkage had been struck; the kinks that needed ironing out.

After a reasonable amount of time, they returned to their phones. Each displayed a ticking digital clock. The various acts had been apportioned a minimum time frame. Should these time frames be exceeded, the cost of continuation would be charged in minute-long increments, with the going rate per extra minute clearly signposted at the point of purchase. These rates, along with the time frames themselves, could also be modified by vendors. The minimum time frame mechanism was in place to ensure that users would always receive a fair rate of pay, even in the event of an unexpectedly short-lived job.

Veronica's screen displayed a red emergency button below the ticking timer. Were this button to be pressed, a line of white would set about encircling it. Once fully surrounded, the button would connect the phone to the nearest police station. Both Annie and Veronica had agreed that such a contingency was essential. The hope was that Pimple – through the power of transparency – would quickly root out the most heinous punters. But the sorting process would inevitably take time, and perhaps pain, too.

The *Help* button notifications existed simply to inform the police of an incident, its location, and the names of those involved. They contained no information about the app or its creators.

The accumulation of paid-for time could be halted only by Veronica, the vendor. A white line ringed its way around the timer when she pressed. It connected at the summit, completing the exchange. Annie received an electronic receipt for £260, as the act had lasted a mere twelve minutes. Veronica received an electronic notification of payment.

Both notifications could be analysed in granular fashion, if desired. Such a homing in would display – again in the name of transparency – a breakdown of the payment, which was divided into *Agreed rate of exchange*, *Overtime* and *Facilitation fee*.

Pimple was to charge a two per cent matchmaking fee on all transactions. The toll had been kept deliberately low – enough only to cover the network's operating costs. Annie had pushed for three per cent, in case of a rapid scaling, but had been haggled down by Veronica, who had said that she could not live with even the smallest risk of profiting from their endeavours. Both women had lived comfortably since cashing in on the acquisition of Millennial Credit; they could afford their altruism.

So it was that Pimple's premier transaction – a non-event, as it happened – was completed. The pair's notices of payment also offered each woman the chance to bestow a star rating of between one and five. Annie fired the first shot.

'Five stars for you, VC,' she said.

'And for you, Miss O'Mahony,' said Veronica.

'Well, I think we deserve a drink, don't you?'

Veronica turned to her friend in thinly concealed alarm.

'It's fine, Ron,' said Annie. 'It's just a drink.'

'OK,' replied Veronica, after a moment's hesitation. 'If you're sure. The Plume of Feathers?'

'Another fine idea, VC!' roared Annie. 'You're full of them these days.'

The two women wandered over to the nearby pub. It was a loud, dank-smelling place. There was a peculiar assortment of snacks spread along the bar-top – the sort that can only be found in ageing British pubs. They found themselves a corner.

'I'll get these,' said Veronica.

'Don't be absurd! The flag's been flown.'

That was what Annie always said when laying claim to the right to buy a round of drinks. The mannerism harked back to a tour that she had once taken of the retired HMY *Britannia*, in the Port of Leith in

Edinburgh, some ten years before. The many stately rooms and cabins aboard the yacht had housed a spectacular array of silverware, rarity and titbit. There was a whale's rib-bone. There was a hand-carved wooden shark from Pitcairn Island that had been signed by descendants of the famous HMS *Bounty* mutineers. There was, to quote the audio guide, *the glittering head of a Thai God* mounted on a wall.

In the officers' mess had been a wonderful item called the Gin Pennant. It was a miniature flagpole, made of sterling silver, with a tiny silken red flag attached. Said flag was raised by an officer to indicate his intention to pick up the next round of drinks. This had stuck in Annie's brain, as so often things did. Those who knew her well knew also what she meant whenever she talked of hoisting, flying, or raising the flag.

They drank a glass of burgundy each, talking of times past. Annie did the bulk of the talking. Her eyes gleamed, her arms flew. The wine seemed not to have the slightest effect upon her. Far more potent was the success of the app's test-run. Money was flowing in the veins of the Pimple network, and her heart beat faster for it.

7

The Fruitless To-and-Fro

Warren walked alongside a flustered-looking Detective David Duffin. He was a portly man, with thinning hair and a kindly face. His clear spectacles were seated a little too far down his nose, and he had a mouth like a small beak. He didn't look a great deal like a police officer at all; rather, he looked like a man in police-themed fancy dress. The pair strode together along a low-lit hospital ward. Duffin clutched a clipboard under one arm.

'What's her condition?' enquired Warren.

'Stable,' said David. 'She'll recover. She's been talking, but the details have been pretty scant so far.'

'Is she awake now?'

'Looks like it,' answered David, swerving left into a private room.

A woman in her early twenties was seated on the white bed on top of the sheets. She was on the phone, but hurriedly hung up as the two men entered. Her face was an autumnal mural, her black skin stained with a mixture of mustards and purples. One of her eyes was all but closed. Her top lip was fattened at the corner, bulging with coagulated blood. She wore a cast on her wrist that extended up towards her elbow; the bruising beneath was evident.

David approached. 'Sasha, how are you feeling?'

He extended a hand. She shook it limply, looking puzzled.

'My apologies,' said David. 'We spoke soon after your arrival here. You may not remember. I'm Detective Duffin, and this is my colleague DCI Beckett.'

Warren nodded courteously. Sasha regarded the two men warily.

David continued in his airy Midlands accent. 'Sasha, we'd like to ask you some questions about how you came to be here. Would that be OK? We can stop at any time.'

Sasha's wariness mutated into unease, plainer than the patchwork bruising on her cheekbones. 'Yeah,' she slowly answered. 'I mean, I'll tell you what I can, innit. I don't remember much.'

'Of course,' smiled David reassuringly. 'Just do the best you can. We can stop at any time, remember.'

Warren was twitchy. He stood with his hands clasped behind his back, keeping to the background. Better that David orchestrate this careful coaxing of detail. The subject was too raw for Warren. Or perhaps he was too raw. Already he sensed that grating caginess in her and knew pretty well how this would play out. Sasha, beaten to within inches of her life, would not breathe a word about what had happened, about who had perpetrated the act, or the nature of the situation that had preceded it. This was not the business of the police, after all. Such was her training.

'Did you know the man who did this to you?' David's voice was airbrush light.

The reply came ominously quickly. 'No,' said Sasha. 'Never met him before.'

'Did you know his name?' asked David.

She shook her head.

'Could you describe what he looked like? Anything you tell us could be useful.'

Sasha pretended to ponder the man's appearance. 'Tall. He was tall.'

'Hair colour?' asked David, suddenly scribbling on his clipboard. Warren tightened the grip of his right hand around the left.

'Dark.'

'Dark,' repeated David. 'Can you be more specific?'

'No I fucking can't!' she snapped.

'OK,' said David, remarkably poised, treading a fine line between composure and condescension. 'Not a problem. What race was he?'

Sasha looked at him fiercely, her carefully styled eyebrows wriggling closer together. At length, she replied. 'He was white.' Pause. 'I think.'

'We're wasting our time here, David,' hissed Warren, unclasping his hands.

'Warren, please…' pleaded the portly detective.

'Fuck off then!' yelled the troubled woman. 'What are you gonna do to help me anyway, hey? What the fuck are you gonna do?'

Warren shaped to respond, anger rising. He could no longer stymie it. He'd done so too many times before. Why must these wretched women be so reluctant to help themselves? He knew the answer, of course, but still it pained him.

David – now tasked with managing two parties in turmoil – remained calm, staying his colleague's outburst with a raised hand. 'We want to help, Sasha. Truly,' he said. 'But to do that we need you to tell us as much as you possibly can about the man who attacked you.'

Sasha looked directly at Warren, her eyes popping with a kind of mindless hostility. Warren returned her gaze with equal ferocity. He was angry with her. He knew it to be wrong of him, blinkered, child-ish even, and yet he couldn't help himself – such was his exasperation at having to endure yet another fruitless to-and-fro.

'There's nothing else,' breathed the vitriolic woman. 'You get me? Nothing else.'

In all likelihood, she too, on some deeply buried level of her soul, knew that these men were not deserving of her enmity. But where else was she free to rant and rave? Warren breathed deep. He knew the cause was lost.

'Have it your way,' he said, his voice flat and gravelly. He swivelled on the heels of his pointy Oxfords and swept towards the door, slamming an open palm into the wall on his way out.

'Warren. Wait!' David's voice came echoing along the corridor, but Warren was undeterred. He scarcely broke stride as he exited the ward through the hefty double doors. By the time David had caught up to him, he already had a cigarette lit and was slumped against a low wall in the car park, some way from the hospital entrance.

'Warren,' began David, breathless and dishevelled.

'She wasn't going to talk, David,' said Warren, pre-empting the rebuke, puffing smoke lazily into the air. 'They never talk.'

David laid a hand upon the wall, slouching a little. 'Since when do you smoke?' he wheezed.

Warren shrugged.

David sighed. 'We have a duty to these women, boss. If they don't want to help, they don't want to help. We have to be patient. We have to cajole them into co-operating. Hasn't Sasha seen enough of men who can't control their tempers?'

Warren stayed silent, staring blankly through the smoke of his cigarette.

'What kind of impression are we making? These women talk!' David insisted.

'Ha! But not to us,' snapped Warren, flicking the cigarette away onto the tarmac.

'We've been doing this for long enough, you and I. We know the score. We know how it works.' David wasn't giving up, but Warren had begun to walk away again. 'You've got to remember who's pulling the strings here, Warren!'

'But I don't know that, do I, David?' barked the detective, turning to face his friend. 'There's Smith, but we can't touch Smith. God knows why we can't, but we can't. We couldn't. And the women won't talk. Or they can't talk. Whichever.' He paused. 'We're getting nowhere.'

'We nearly had him once.'

'Years ago.' Warren flapped his arms, helpless and exasperated. 'Years ago. And it fell apart in a way that says to me that we're not supposed to get him. That we'll never get him.'

David had no rebuttal. There could be no denying the sickening loss that both men had endured when Emerson Smith had last wriggled free of his comeuppance. Words had been whispered from on high, or so it had seemed. Evidence had been called into question. The case, ensnared in a web of bureaucracy, had collapsed.

'I'm tired, David,' said Warren, absently. 'I'm always tired. I can't keep chasing ghosts. I'll see you tomorrow.'

David did not follow him this time, instead calling out a few time-worn words of encouragement, as was his way. Warren had always found David curiously and incurably upbeat, given his line of work, and impossibly patient, too. Like a noiseless valley lake, he never seemed depleted. Warren envied him that.

Warren wandered mindlessly down Westminster Bridge Road, and on past St. George's Cathedral towards the outskirts of Elephant and Castle. His actions simmered in the back of his brain. He took a deliberately roundabout route home, waiting for his thoughts to fizzle out, even sitting for a while in Newington Gardens – one of those scuffed-up bits of London greenery with an overly grandiose title.

He planted the back of his skull upon a cold park bench, and tried to imagine his body draining away through the hundred little holes. The sky above was obscured by cloud and various wisps of other vaporous clutter. Here and there a fleeting star shone through, soon to be blotted out. On the branches above clung a few tenacious browning leaves; their siblings were scattered around the ground.

Warren's body ached. His muscles were in open revolt. That great heaviness still clung to him, like the gaseous slag above the city. Rarely had he felt such defeat.

8

Beyond Deference

Elena glanced at herself in the rear-view mirror. The eyes of John Canty were waiting. She quickly averted her gaze, settling instead into looking idly out of the passenger window.

Once again she had been summoned. The balding driver was another of Smith's men. He could often be seen in Westminster or in Soho, watching over the girls while keeping an eye out for bad punters. He was a big and simple man, prone to sudden outbursts of rage, but often unable to articulate their stimuli. Barbed-wire tattoos crept upwards on his neck like ivy up a thick tree trunk.

Elena hadn't seen Mike since she had been called in by Smith. His calls and messages had been left unanswered. It had been a hellish few weeks out on the streets since. And now she was returning – she could only assume – to the scene of her last encounter with Smith. Her stomach jostled uncomfortably as they turned a corner. She tugged anxiously on the sleeves of her slim-fitted jumper. The street lamps blurred as the sedan sped by. The roads were quiet.

It soon became clear that they were not headed to Smith's office. Elena panicked, and risked a question.

'Where are we going?' she asked shakily.

'You'll see,' answered John, forebodingly; Elena knew not to press the issue.

She laid her head against the window and tried to clear her mind. The buildings began to thin a little, and the night sky opened up. They were heading well clear of the city centre. The rows of houses had transformed into warehouses, plants and distilleries. Great steel vats and refineries reared. Rotator blades lined the tops of high stone walls, and the gateways were spined and spiked.

The vehicle veered suddenly into a bay. A pair of men emerged from the shadows, one lifting up a heavy latch and swinging the gate open. The car tailed the other man slowly towards what seemed to be a warehouse, stopping outside a truck-sized entrance. An eerie, greenish light glowed from inside.

'Get out,' commanded John.

Elena obeyed. As she moved robotically into the poorly lit space, familiar faces loomed into view. There was 'Skinny' Summers, and there Tom Marsden. Men she knew well. Five or six of them in total, it was hard to be sure.

The warehouse itself was a shell. A few walkways clung to the high metal walls, but none of them seemed to lead anywhere. The long criss-crossed windows were green with the build-up of some weed or fungus, which contorted the starlight on entry.

Soon she glimpsed a man of average height, with slicked-back hair and an ugly, tangled beard. Emerson Smith watched her approach with a languid malice in his posture. Elena became aware of the proximity of her escorts: Summers and Marsden were flanking her; John remained ahead. To the casual observer she might have appeared rather important, being convoyed around in this way.

John's broad form gave way to a grisly scene. A man in a suit was sitting beside Smith on a steel chair. He wore what looked like the clothes of a businessman, though the tie had been twisted out of shape, and a sleeve of the navy blazer had been ripped at the elbow. A black sack was tied around his neck, obscuring his face from view. The closer Elena and her entourage drew, the louder his whimpers became. He was turning one of his booted feet this way and that, swivelling on the heel. As the approach party halted, Smith laid a hand softly on his left shoulder. His body jumped.

'Elena, my dear,' said Smith, his voice unnervingly even. 'So kind of you to join us. I do hope you weren't too busy.'

'I wasn't,' answered Elena, instinctively pandering.

'Curious, given the time,' replied Smith, consulting his garish gold wristwatch. Caught out, Elena moved to explain herself, but Smith continued. 'Not to worry. I didn't bring you here to check up on you.'

He strode towards her, grabbed her by the elbow and walked her over to the man in the seat. He placed a hand on each of her shoulders and stared into her eyes. An overpowering smell of cologne entered Elena's nostrils and lodged itself there. A familiar smell. Smith's beady eyes were perfectly still.

'I have a very important question for you, Elena. The man in this seat represents a threat to my business, and, incidentally to you, and to all the girls working on the streets. Elena, I'm going to take his hood off now. I simply need you to tell me two things. Number one: do you recognise his face? And number two – which is of course contingent on your first answer – where from? Do you understand, Elena?'

Elena's shoulders trembled beneath his hands. There was nothing to do but to play the game.

'Yes, boss.'

'That's my girl!' beamed Smith. Without delay, he whipped the hood away.

Elena's eyes widened. Her body convulsed. She knew him. A man whose skin looked like it had been drawn too tightly across the bony structure of his face. Whose rank, limp hair flopped down across his brow, partially obscuring his eyes. She had seen Sasha climb into his car a few nights back down a dingy lane in Marylebone. She had then visited Sasha the next day in hospital, where she found her friend badly mauled, as if savaged by a dog.

And here was the dog, slumped sideways in a sorry state. Blood dripped from a cut to his forehead, but it was clear that while fear had soaked him through, he had not yet sustained much in the way of bodily harm; it was clear also that it was for Elena to decide whether he would. But all these thoughts came too quick, and in among them was an impulsive anger that would not be overruled. As the man's lips shaped as if to plead, she spoke.

'I know him,' she exclaimed, and then, more quietly: 'He picked up Sasha in Marylebone on Thursday.' Smith straightened, considering the answer. Then he turned to his men and nodded.

The first punch caught the man square on the jaw, dislodging the far side of his face with a shuddering jolt. Elena gasped, but saw no more. Emerson had taken a hold of her and was wheeling her around and away from the scene.

'No need for you to witness that unpleasantness, my dear.' He spoke the words softly into her ear. 'I thank you for your honesty, Elena. It's so important that we root out filth like him. I can't in good faith send you off to work in the knowledge that men like that are prowling around the alleyways now, can I? What kind of man would that make me?'

The awful cracks and groans persisted in the background. Guilt was flooding into Elena's head, displacing her fear. She had condemned him. He might die tied to that chair. Did he deserve that?

Smith, apparently sensing her turmoil, intervened. 'You mustn't blame yourself for his fate, Elena. He pays a necessary penance. You've no doubt seen the state he left sweet Sasha in. We can't have that. Can't have it.'

They were out in the air now. A smell like rust wafted by. John lingered nearby, like a crudely carved totem pole. Once again Emerson fixed her with a mad and searching stare, and grasped her shoulders.

'Any man that hurts you, or hurts Sasha, or hurts any of my girls, will suffer ten times what he's inflicted,' he said. His left eye was twitching. 'I promise you that, Elena. I will tear that man to nothing. I'll send him home broken-boned and spitting teeth. And all who see him will know: you do not hurt my girls.' He spoke ferociously: calmly, but with an intensity that chilled Elena to the core. After a short silence, she realised what he was waiting for.

'Thank you, boss. Thank you,' she half-whispered. 'We know we're safe with you.'

And like that, a smile broke across his face. He released her and stood back, still beaming.

'Marvellous. Don't you forget it,' he said, wagging a finger in her direction.

Smith then adjusted his check jacket with a shake of the shoulders, and tugged at his shirt cuffs. Elena thought of herself, tugging at her own sleeves.

'Duty calls,' was his farewell, accompanied with a wink. He strode back into the warehouse, where cries of pain were still reverberating.

Again the guilt returned. John was ushering her back into the vehicle she had arrived in some ten minutes earlier. It felt a lot longer. The car was soon going again. Elena had a feeling of being a long way away.

'Boss says you don't need to work no more tonight,' said John suddenly, simply. 'I'll take you home.'

The blunt declaration brought Elena back. It was not relief but rage that built up inside her. The evil of Emerson Smith was hard to put into words, but it certainly couldn't be confined to the word pimp.

A half-night off in twenty.

'Great,' she said aloud, unintentionally. But there was no danger. John was too thick to detect her tone. He just grunted, and drove Elena to her lodgings, as he had been instructed to do.

9

Customer Acquisition

The uneven tapping of stilettos pierced the silent passageway. A lone woman walked an awkward kind of catwalk between the overrunning bins. Annie rose up out of the six-inch high heels like the stem of an ungainly plant. She wore a short red skirt, and a trimly fitted leather jacket that belonged to a friend. Her hair was its usual unruly mass of twists and turns. She wore a thick face of makeup that looked as though it had been applied by an unpractised hand. She drew a deep breath before stepping out of the shadow of the shop-row crevice.

'I'm bloody freezing,' she said in a shuddering voice. 'This jacket of yours – a little on the skimpy side, no?'

'Hence my advising you against wearing it.' The scolding came crackling to life in the right side of Annie's head, emanating from a small black earpiece.

'Authenticity, Veronica!' spluttered Annie through the cold. 'That's the key.' She folded her arms and gyrated on the spot, mustering up the courage to exit the wind-sheltered alley. 'Right then. On with the show.'

She was now on Wardour Street, the neon-lit road that cleaves bustling Soho town in two. Taxis zipped this way and that. Groups of giggling girls and pucker-faced boys flocked in and out of a nearby gay bar, in the window of which bounced a bare male bottom. Great round men in long overcoats roared with laughter in the smoking areas of old English pubs, which looked as though they'd been plucked from a fairy tale. Every other pub seemed to have incorporated the word 'King' or 'Queen' into its title.

A few quieter restaurants were slotted away here and there, from within which diners observed the outside world with a faint disdain.

The smoky air that filled the narrow street carried a kind of barely detectable pulse. Sugar clung to cocktail glass rims like stubble to a chin. The traffic flowed in only one direction, up towards Oxford Street.

Plenty of people were loitering, but Annie soon realised – as she expected to – that some loitered more purposefully than others. These were the people she was interested in. They gave themselves away through their dress, primarily. Everything was just a little too short, too overspilled by flesh. Their makeup was overdone too – as was her own. Indeed, they looked on the whole as peculiar as Annie did in the chilly winter's night. She was pleased.

There were other clues too. A blonde woman, reclined against a lamppost up ahead, was overdoing her nonchalance. Further along the road, beneath the chain-hung potted plants of a French inn, a thick-bodied woman, apparently lost in thought, cast furtive glances in the direction of the oncoming traffic.

The greatest giveaway was the fact that each of Annie's suspects faced inwards, never for a moment turning their backs to the busy road. Annie was in high spirits as she walked towards the top end of Wardour Street. A tingle of excitement made her shiver, a feat that the cold had yet to accomplish. She felt as one who stands upon the brink of rebellion.

Further back down Wardour Street, deep within the throng of bodies, a few of Annie's suspects had already clambered into vehicles. As they did, the snaking line of women adjusted, each one sliding casually a little further from the top of the street. The stage was perfectly set.

'Green light,' said Annie. 'I repeat, green light.'

Veronica's eyes would doubtless be rolling, but a reply came soon enough. 'Roger.'

Annie positioned herself between what appeared to be a Soho walk-up and a dirty old dry-cleaner's, hugging herself against the cold. Trumpets were sounding in some far-off pocket of thought. A great shift was afoot; she could feel it. Like an urban chameleon, she assumed the posture of her peers, none of whom seemed to be paying her the slightest attention. They were, unsurprisingly, far too focused on the evening's work. No sign of any skulking enforcers either, much to Annie's relief.

Soon enough she saw what she had been waiting for. A low black vehicle was picking its way slowly up the road. A series of scantily dressed women sidled over to the car window, one after the other. But each time, after what looked to be a brief exchange between the driver and the would-be passenger, it nudged onwards, only to stop again as it drew level with the next bachelorette. Unlikely to be an uncommonly discerning customer, thought Annie – more likely that this was her man.

The exact words that passed between the mystery driver and the succession of disregarded women could not yet be made out, but the car was now almost within earshot. Only two women stood between Annie and her own bite at the proverbial apple. The nearest was some thirty yards away and soon enough the vehicle had crept level with her, a trail of puzzlement and irritation left in its wake.

A short mixed-race woman with a loftily set ponytail strutted boldly up to the car door. No doubt she was aware of the apparent pickiness of its director and had decided to meet that choosiness with bravado. The window lowered. There was an exchange of words and the proud vixen recoiled in apparent confusion. The window rolled up, and the car rolled on.

Annie detached herself from the shop wall and ventured forth towards the gutter, like a stork between reeds. She had nothing of the swagger of her predecessor, who appeared to be observing her jittery advance, condescension smeared across her face. *Perfect*, thought Annie, stilling herself upon the pavement edge. The unwieldy bird was poised to strike.

The car slowed to a stop in front of her, which was in itself sufficient to hoist the eyebrows of the watching woman. The window wound down and there loomed the familiar and flustered face of Peter Froome. His sunken eyes were more panda-like than ever. His forehead gleamed with sweat, and his lightly seated hair was unusually dishevelled. He looked as pale as a sheet – positively ill, in fact. Annie bent at the knees to peer through the window. She widened her eyes, drawing forth a question.

'Are you on Pimple?' he asked, sheepishly.

'Louder!' she hissed between her teeth.

'Are you on Pimple?' repeated Peter, unnaturally loudly. 'The app?'

The sentence was at odds with his elegant Etonian accent. Annie rolled her eyes, but nodded vigorously. Mechanically, Peter stretched out a hand and caressed her cheek with the backs of his fingers, which were shaking. He then beckoned her in with a flick of the wrist, in line with his instructions.

She trotted around the vehicle, making sure to throw a glance in the direction of the baffled vixen as she did. As Annie's suitability became clear, the short woman promptly span upon her heels and clopped off in the direction of her closest colleague, her large hooped earrings flapping as she went. No doubt she went to report her findings: that a stumbling, tangle-haired woman had been found worthy, and that her comprehension of this 'Pimple' – an app, by the sounds of things – seemed to be the deciding factor. Annie grinned.

'How was that?' asked Peter, as she clambered into the car.

'Drive, man!' she instructed.

He mumbled an apology and pressed his foot to the accelerator, bringing them out onto the more spacious hubbub of Oxford Street.

Annie settled, exhaling lengthily. 'That, my dear, was perfect.'

'I don't believe they're especially used to rejection,' murmured Peter. 'Quite the deluge of indignation!'

'I should hope so too,' replied Annie, beaming. Her heart was thundering. 'A credit to your execution, Mr Froome. I assume you're getting this, Ron? Mission accomplished, dear girl!'

'Bravo. On to Shorts Gardens then,' came the crackling voice of Veronica.

'She says bravo,' said Annie, leaning over to her chauffeur. 'And that we must press on. So sorry again that I couldn't persuade Ron to play the pick-up girl, dear.' She rubbed Peter's shoulder in mock sympathy.

'Now, see here…' he blurted, as Veronica chided her through the earpiece.

Annie flopped back into her seat and clapped her hands together, laughing heartily. 'Oh come now, you two. I'm only having a bit of fun!'

'Yes, well,' said Peter, awkwardly. 'Shorts Gardens. Onwards.'

'Onwards!' cried Annie.

They soon arrived at the Drury Lane end of Shorts Gardens, another one-way road teeming with temptresses. Annie bundled herself out of the vehicle. Peter wheeled away to await his orders. Annie paced an awkward path along the narrow road, catching the eyes of the odd curious loiterer. She waited at the roundabout by Cambridge Court and gave the all-clear. Again the creeping car and its seemingly insatiable conductor began to trundle up the road, dismissing women to left and right as it went. Again, Annie, a peculiar-looking, last-chance saloon, ticked the fussy driver's boxes. Again this 'Pimple' – whatever it was – appeared to make the difference.

The pair repeated this same process on many different one-way streets in central London that night. The only hiccups came when women – desperate to defend a hard-earned pedestal – reacted aggressively to Annie's incursion, and chased or barked her away in territorial fashion. But Annie made no attempt to resist such efforts; if her presence proved the cause of outright animosity, then the exercise was null. Instead she aimed to be regarded with something closer to casual interest, and some way towards suspicion.

By the following evening, a Saturday, each of the visited streets was plastered with Pimple paraphernalia. Every telephone box pane was stickered. Every lamppost had been postered. Leaflets were strewn in their dozens along the pavements.

Each bit of blurb read the same: 'Take control. Try Pimple.'

The words were emblazoned in a chic white font on a bright red background. Below them there was a small square barcode; scanning this led to a webpage from which the Pimple app could be downloaded. It was compatible with all manner of mobile devices. There had been a great deal of toing and froing over whether or not to provide more in the way of explanatory text on the leaflets. Ultimately, Annie and Veronica had decided that a minimalist approach was best: a degree of mystery, coupled with the intrigue of the previous night's chicanery, comingled as a tasty bait. The download page itself provided more explanation.

It was an unconventional approach to marketing, Annie had to admit. Then again, this was to be a most unconventional business.

She and Veronica sat together that Saturday night at Annie's house in Fulham with a laptop open. A few nibbles had been laid out, but were largely untouched. Annie soon began pacing the floorboards. The evening was still young.

'Just one download,' she said, continuing to wander around the open-plan living room. 'I'd be happy with a single download.'

'Patience,' said Veronica, flicking through a book.

'I'm being perfectly patient,' snapped Annie. 'I'm just saying that I'd like to get at least one download.'

'We may, we may not,' said Veronica, in a matter-of-fact tone. Annie threw her hands in the air and walked over to the window, which looked out onto the street below. The minutes dragged on; the screen lay dormant.

'We're a pair of fools, Ron,' declared Annie after a while, sitting down next to her friend.

Veronica looked up from her book. 'Perhaps,' she answered. 'But I suspect most worthy endeavours start out a little foolish.'

Annie smiled. 'I said I'd see Oliver next week. Just to catch up,' she said quietly.

'That's great, Annie,' said Veronica cautiously. 'When did you last see one another?'

'Not since it all went tits up!' she replied. 'There's no feeling anymore. No love, no anger. I suppose I just want him to know that I'm fine now. God knows he's been checking in on me often enough.'

Veronica looked on the verge of saying something, but no words came; she seemed to be struggling to find the right combination. 'I think it's fantastic that you're comfortable enough to see him,' she said at last. 'It was such a difficult time. The way it all stacked up, with MILC, and…' she tailed off.

Annie didn't look up. Her mind was with her lost child, as it always was whenever she thought of Oliver.

'I'm so proud of you for how far you've come,' said Veronica.

Annie smiled again. She had written several poems about the loss of her son, but no longer liked any of them. The best of the bad bunch was entitled '2009':

A mean gale blows.
The father fiddles a match.
Caterpillar weeds crawl, synthetic petals sag.
A bedraggled bear plays witness,
Chewing on the rain.
Snap, soundless fizzle.
The candlelight is conjured.
The mother backs into the wind,
Sheltering the little light.
A ring of flesh is formed:
The family in full, frozen in a storm.
Life's wick bows, if but a bit.
A kitsch mill spits.
Jumbled-up chimes jangle out of time.
An old doll topples over.
Tears are wept and swept away, fresh from the cornea.
Sentences half-strung are spun into the sky.
The party submits, and splits,
The candlelight quits –
Committed unto the honeycombed heath –
Not alive long enough to die.

The soft ding of an inbound email sounded. The women lurched into life; Annie's finger found the mouse-pad first. Neither could quite believe their eyes. A download. A solitary, pioneering, glittering download. From Lisa, sweet Lisa. They turned to one another. Annie roared triumphantly and threw her arms around Veronica. Cries of 'I knew it, I knew we'd get one!' rang out, and soon enough a bottle cork had been popped.

Lisa, as it turned out, was the first of many. Several dozen women downloaded the mysterious Pimple app on that fateful night in London. Within weeks, the network was alive, crawling with patrons like termites in a mound. Admittedly the first of these downloads were exploratory in nature; it would take time for them to blossom into engaged users. But that hardly mattered for now.

Annie had always maintained – when nattering away to Veronica – that the truest reflection of having satisfied a dire need was the sudden materialisation of scale. So had it been with Millennial Credit, so it now was with Pimple.

Disintermediation – perhaps the defining word in her lexicon – was under way once more.

PART II

Revolution

10

Virgin Clients

Elena sat on the edge of her bed, pulling on her jeans. She stood and straightened out her long dark hair in the mirror. The glass pane was bordered with little lights. She had looked fuller in the face lately, and there were no bags beneath her eyes. She looked not only healthier, but happier, too.

'That was amazing, baby.' Her client spoke in a drawl. His name was Thomas, one of her regulars. He was buttoning up a silly-looking pin-striped shirt. He had a slight paunch and a generally scruffy look to him. He was harmless.

'I need you to leave now,' said Elena, forcefully, repositioning a pair of earrings. 'I have another appointment soon.'

'Right. Right you are!' replied Thomas, leaping into action, throwing on a tatty brown jumper and stuffing his feet into a pair of deck shoes. Elena gently chivvied him in the direction of the door, where he turned for a goodbye kiss. She could have done without it.

'I'll see you again soon,' said Thomas, attempting to fondle her chin.

'I hope so,' replied Elena.

Thomas made to kiss her on the lips. She countered with a kiss to the cheek. The door closed between them.

Elena turned the lock and bolted the door shut. Tired, she wandered into the compact kitchen and slouched against the oven. She withdrew her mobile phone from her pocket – she was never far from it these days – and pressed her thumb to the glowing *P*.

Thomas trusted her to take care of their business. She had earned that trust, not only through their direct dealings, but through her stellar track record of dealings on the Pimple network in general. Her 4.9 star rating was unheard of, and worth its weight in gold.

The app displayed a meter, which had registered four minutes and twelve seconds of overtime. That meant that the transaction had run for nearly a full twenty minutes. It didn't matter to Elena in the case of Thomas – inoffensive as he was. It just meant an extra £80 on top of the £300 that the allotted fifteen minutes would have cost him.

He regularly exceeded the quarter-hour mark, and Elena did nothing to discourage it. She did not hate him in the way that she had hated some clients. She was indifferent to him. He brought the cash in. For the sake of some reasonably tame shuffling around and a few sweet nothings, he came back time and time again. More importantly, though, he seemed to be almost entirely inelastic.

She signed off on the completion of their business, giving Thomas the customary five-star rating. How he would glow. She soon received the same rating back, accompanied some five minutes later by a message expressing his desire to see her again soon. Elena replied with the words, 'Me too,' and added a heart-shaped icon for good measure.

The notification of payment arrived. More money banked. She'd soon have enough to begin a new life. To leave the city, perhaps even leave the country altogether. She could set up a small shop, or travel. One more year of work.

The sex became more bearable by the day. Her days were shorter because the jobs were increasingly lucrative, and the punters were better too. Still not great, of course. But never cruel, and never violent. Such men had been quickly weeded out of the Pimple network.

The evening was early. Elena set about making dinner. The fridge was modestly filled. There were spices in rows above her and a bread bin with a single loaf. It filled her heart with gladness to work in the little kitchen; to feel at home. The kitchen at her former lodgings had been scantly stocked and shared between many women – women who were closely policed.

Elena was one of the first women to have picked up a little red Pimple leaflet on the streets of Soho some two months before. She downloaded the app out of curiosity but had quickly – more quickly than most – grasped its potential. And she knew, somehow she knew, that Smith and others like him would fail to comprehend that potential at first glance. Or perhaps they would refuse to. Either way, she knew what had to be done. The promise of escape had arisen; she had taken a hold of it and vanished.

She'd found the shoddiest of one-room apartments to rent in east London and had paid a deposit with what little change she had managed to hide away. Her getaway fund: enough only to cover a few months' rent. She had gambled on Pimple. It had paid off.

There were no chips implanted in the necks of Emerson Smith's girls; that they were *his* girls in itself was enough. It was well known that he was the loosest of London's pimps when it came to controlling his girls, but it was exactly that looseness that confirmed him as the worst of them. His rule was so complete that many women mistook it for care.

But not Elena. She had never fallen for it. In fact, she felt more oppressed for being so apparently able, but so helplessly unable, to escape him. That he had noticed her fling with Mike was evidence enough that Smith's eyes and ears were everywhere. And what could they hope to do without him anyway – the girls whose lives he had marshalled so carefully for so long? Where could they go? The women knew the answer as well as he did: there was nothing, and there was nowhere.

Elena knew it better than most. That was why Pimple – an aggressively alternative way of doing things – had so suddenly inspired her to risk everything.

The act of her escape had not been dramatic. She had gone out to work on the cold streets of Westminster, as she had done so many times before. Several kerb-crawlers passed her by without her even noticing. She was lost to the idea of freedom. After a while Sasha, who had begun the evening with her, came back from a job to find her friend still rooted to the spot in thought, looking like a statue from a bygone age.

'Elena,' she had said, softly. 'You gotta work, girl. There's nothing for it.'

And as if snapped from a trance, Elena had then looked at her friend in so mystifying a way that Sasha shrank back a little.

'There might be,' she'd said.

She'd then walked deep, deep into the night until she felt convinced that she had not been followed, and from the next day began a new life.

But the eyes of Emerson Smith were indeed everywhere, and there would be more of them soon. Elena didn't leave the flat much, and concealed her face when she did. Soon, if they hadn't already, every London-based pimp would wise up to the disruptive threat that was posed by Pimple, she was sure of it.

Elena had urged Sasha and others among her peers to run away with her – but they wouldn't listen. Some didn't even want to be free; they didn't know what Elena meant by it. A large number of women had signed up to the app since its emergence, but it was hardest for the worst-off women, and it was only getting harder.

Elena made herself a steaming beef stew: a small amount of meat in the juices of tomatoes and peppers, with spices and herbs. The smell of cinnamon filled the room. She broke into the loaf and dunked the bread in the sauce as she ate. Ordinarily she would eat in front of the TV – a dusty old box someone had left behind. It worked well enough, and she was trying to get into a few of the many soap operas and talk shows that seemed to dominate British screens.

Her phone chirped. A man had requested the pleasure of her company. She stretched a sheet of cling film across the open pot and stowed what remained of the stew in the fridge. She then looked at the bleating phone.

A man bearing the initials *RC* was on the prowl. His details would be picked up by any vendors within a pre-set distance. It was for these women to choose whether or not to negotiate with him. *RC*'s display would feature only those women who chose to engage. But a quick glance at the *RC* profile suggested he might not have much luck. He displayed a rating of a little under two stars.

Elena, still intrigued by the ins and outs of the technology, homed in on the *RC* profile. There was an exclamation mark in the comment box beneath his name, suggestive of sinister depths. There were only two reviews. The first said he could be rough. The second simply read: *Avoid. Horrid.*

The words were a black mark on the profile, tattooed into cyberspace. They were also invisible to *RC* himself. He knew little of the level of disclosure that he had committed to when he signed up to the app. A great many eyes were at this very moment considering him, gauging his suitability. And all the while he felt nothing but the prickling of his hormones.

Elena rejected the undesirable *RC*, vanishing the job listing from her dashboard. She then decided to do what she had been meaning to do for some time. She went into her Pimple preferences and fiddled with the filters. From now on, she would only work with the best, odd though it was to think of them like that. She instructed Pimple to hide all requests from men with fewer than four stars. After all, her own high-star rating gave her the right to be fussy. Why lower herself to the scummier end of the spectrum when there were plenty of punters to be had at both ends, and in the middle?

A strange kind of thrill filled her. She returned the phone to her pocket, nestled down on the sofa and turned on the old TV. The concept of control had been so alien for so long. She had been a teenager when she had left home. The idea now, not only of rejecting a prospective customer, but also of implementing her own set of rules, was an audacious leap into the unfamiliar. And as a prisoner might shield her eyes from the sun after years spent underground, so too Elena took gingerly to her newfound autonomy. But the feeling was a stirring one.

Before long she found herself losing patience with the TV and once again turning to the app. There was a monitoring button that stored the details of every one of her jobs. The dashboard kept tabs on her earnings to date, average payout per job, fees paid, and so on.

By digging a little deeper, Elena was also able to pull up her earnings per minute, worked out in relation to a 'Pimple Earnings Benchmark' – which represented the historical average for users of the app. The graph ran from the date of the app's birth right through to the present. Both lines followed upward trajectories, but Elena's soared high above the average.

She continued to explore. Then suddenly she caught sight of herself, as though from across the room. She saw the feeling of satisfaction, perhaps even pride. She dropped the phone by her side. Tears sprang to her eyes. The past month had been a frenzy. She hadn't allowed herself the luxury of emotional response. Her tears were of relief and joy on the one hand, but of anger on the other.

Here she was, free to leave London, free to do as she pleased. But she had chosen to continue to work as a prostitute, justifying the decision through much improved conditions, and through the vague idea of needing more money. She was afraid. She had been for a very long time. The phone that lay beside her repelled her in that moment. She felt ashamed for having let herself get carried away with her newfound freedoms. *They are far, far from enough*, she reminded herself. It was all just a stopgap.

Elena slept roughly that night. Her dreams were vivid. She woke several times in fits of panic. It was never clear to her quite why; it was the kind of distress that comes with forgetfulness, only this feeling ran deeper.

She sat in her bed, slumped against the wall of the small room – which was perfectly dark. Her phone was about the only thing in the room that could be detected. She wanted to look at it as much as she wanted to throw it from the window.

She picked it up, and thumbed her way again into world of Pimple. Within it, women worked, earned and connected. Elena imagined that she could hear them all, toing and froing industriously.

She rolled down the homepage. Right at the bottom she discovered a *Community* button. She had never seen it before. The button led to a platform on which customer reviews could be written. There was also a tool for keeping tabs on repeat customers. After all, Thomas was harmless today, but who might he be tomorrow? Elena marvelled at the thing. The architect – whoever he or she was – had considered everything, down to the minutest of details.

Then a terrifying thought occurred. Who indeed was the architect? Elena had not considered this before. The face of Smith and every one of his thugs flashed through her mind. Could it be? No. She dismissed the idea outright. She would not allow her newfound freedoms to be corrupted like that.

Elena noticed that another tab with the title *Forum* was hovering neatly in the lower regions of her screen. Intrigued – and in need of distraction – she entered. What she found was a dashboard teeming with message threads. The first was entitled: *How do u know if some1 is a wrongn if they got no rating?* There were seventeen responses; it was clearly a popular topic.

I've been unfairly charged for overtime. How do I claim a refund? Ah, a customer-led conversation. These were rarer. As she scrolled, she grew more and more amazed at the number of customers, and at the level of their engagement. Few of the commenters were properly named. Most used pseudonyms, many of which were lewd. She supposed this was inevitable.

Elena then spotted an especially popular thread, entitled *Meeting to discuss the Pimple app and how improve it.* The thread was off-limits to customers; only vendors could view its contents. The messages were about *strengthening ties within the community, fair pricing,* and so on. There were even murmurings that the network's creators might be involved. Elena thought that some of the more technical language supported these rumours.

A date and time for the meeting had already been set for 17 November, at midday – a couple days' time – in north London. Women who signed up (a link was available) would receive an invitation from Pimple on the morning of the 17th, which would reveal the venue. *Aha!* Thought Elena. Surely the hand of the creator at play. But did that make her more or less keen to attend?

In the end, her curiosity won out. She clicked the link and waited. She noted that there was no need to enter contact information; Pimple knew exactly who she was. She felt vulnerable. She lay down. Sleep came swiftly, mercifully.

Over the next few days Elena swayed between whether or not to go to the gathering. She continued to use the app in the meantime, but with increased caution – as if at any moment Emerson Smith might appear on the other end of it, ready to collect his dues.

'Should I not use the rod?' she could hear him saying.

By the evening of the 16th, she was resolved. She would go.

The morning came, and with it a message from Pimple, telling her to head for a shared workspace near Old Street. Elena slipped from the block of flats. She had wound a scarf up high around her neck and chin – high enough to chew on. She had pulled a beanie hat down low upon her brow – low enough to look into. She took the Tube to London Bridge and travelled on the Northern Line to Old Street. From there it was a short walk to the location.

Elena walked quickly, shoulders hunched, eyes down. It was a strange sort of area that she passed through, between the City and Shoreditch. She had never been there before. She walked in the shadows of glass towers, but to the north the skyline fell away. The streets were rough, and smelled of the previous night.

Up ahead, a half-dozen men in loosely fitting clothes lounged about the entrance to a barber's shop, talking loudly and smoking. No hair was being cut inside. A group of smart-looking people further ahead were drinking coffee in a box-shaped shop that looked to have been furnished with the wooden remains of a run-down church.

Then Elena reached the venue, and entered.

'Hello there. How may I help you?' asked an enthusiastic woman at the reception desk. She was wearing a flannel shirt and big hooped earrings.

'I'm here for a' – Elena faltered – 'meeting,' she settled on. 'Oh, umm. Sunlight is the best disinfectant.' The app had advised her to speak these words on arrival.

'Fantastic. You're up to the third floor. Room number 12. Lifts are over there. Have a lovely day.' The woman beamed.

Elena moved over to the lifts uneasily. All around her were young men and women, again wearing flannel shirts or t-shirts and frayed jeans. There were lots of overgrown beards and trainers and strangely shaped colourful objects that were not seats, but which were being used for seating. There were long wooden tables and benches that looked like they'd been plucked from a Viking-age mead hall; a large queue was forming at a highly overworked coffee machine.

There was also free craft beer on tap – a much-lauded feature of the offices. Of course, the cost of that beer had been worked into the cost of renting desk-space. And truth be told, there were very few people in the offices who chose to drink beer – craft or otherwise – in the middle of a working day.

Two other women were waiting by the lift controls, both acting as if they hoped the other wouldn't notice her. Elena happily played along. The discomfort deepened when it became clear that they were all heading to the third floor. One was a large-boned, frizzy-haired woman with arms that hung a little lower than they ought to. She wore clunky boots and thick eye makeup and looked like a punk. The other was mixed race, with tightly braided hair and a creased brow – the latter possibly caused by the former. She was bouncing on her toes. They stood in silence as the lift slid upwards.

When the doors opened, the atmosphere changed. They stepped into a corridor that was alive with voices and the clinking of coffee cups – all coming from a long seminar room. A pair of double doors stood open some way along; several women stood nervily outside of the entrance. Within was a human hotchpotch of the most extraordinary variety.

Many of the women – they were all women – looked like Elena, and kept mostly to themselves. They had not touched the refreshments. They appeared both standoffish and fearful, and they mostly fidgeted with their mobiles, trying to look busy.

Then there was another clearly defined set. These women stood in clusters and clutched ceramic coffee cups. They spoke in barely hushed tones about their experiences with the Pimple app. They looked altogether less shabby; some looked positively classy. One was even wearing a blazer.

Finally there were the anomalies, who were tougher to spot: women who clung to the outside of the clusters in listening-only roles. Women who were backed into the wall at such an angle that they might have been propping it up. One in particular was scowling so fiercely that a space had formed around her.

The short woman with the furrowed brow turned to Elena. 'What are we meant to do?'

'I'm not sure,' replied Elena. There seemed to be no focal point for the meeting.

'Well,' continued the woman. 'We may as well take off then.'

But she did not leave. It soon became clear that most of the talk had been about confusion at the lack of structure. And while they puzzled, and while mostly empty threats about leaving flew, more and more women piled into the room, forcing Elena further inside.

There were a few high tables on which lay stacks of printouts. Elena took one. On it was a set of questions, each relating to the Pimple network.

'What's it say?' asked the woman with the creased forehead, who seemed to have latched herself to Elena's side.

'It's a set of questions. Questions about the app,' answered Elena. 'It's signed by Pimple. Says they're listening.'

Elena looked around, hoping for some sign of these mysterious beings. What she found instead was that a number of women had turned to look at her. Her eyes widened in dismay.

The scowling woman from the wall detached herself and spoke. 'Go on,' she said, both fierce and imploring. 'Read them then.'

More and more of the women had turned, encircling Elena as a storm does its eye. She quickly decided that the best thing to do was to read on; refusing would likely cause more trouble. Her slender fingers trembled as she raised the sheet of paper.

'What's good about…'

'Speak up!' a voice interrupted.

Elena redoubled her efforts. 'What's good about Pimple?'

Murmurs rippled across the room. Then came a flurry of answers.

'The freedom!' cried the woman in the quilted blazer, punching a fist in the air.

'Better blokes!' yelled another, low-voiced woman, causing hysterics among those nearby.

The word 'safer' featured in a number of replies. The lack of pimps was another common theme.

'It gives us more control,' called a voice from towards the back. 'It means we pick and choose, not the other way around.' The words were met with grunts of agreement.

'There's nothing good about it,' snapped the woman from the wall, cutting through the commotion. She spoke with venom. 'It's just better than what we had before. We're still hookers. Men still pigs. That ain't changed. Oh, and by the way, there's still some geezer taking my money in the middle.'

'Less money.' Elena could hardly believe her own interjection. She drew breath sharply as though trying to recall the words.

The woman from the wall hoiked up her eyebrows. 'You think any of my money is OK? You think robbery's OK, so long as they don't take too much?'

Elena was – much to her own surprise once more – equipped with an answer. In her fear, she had read the terms and conditions of the app in minute detail.

'They take a two per cent fee. Enough only to keep the network running. They're philanthropists, not pimps.' Her confidence and eloquence intrigued the crowd of women, all the more so because of her Slavic accent.

'And who are you anyway?' barked her interrogator. 'You said it yourself. They're listening. How do we know that *they* ain't *you*?'

Elena floundered slightly, suddenly realising the precariousness of her position. 'I had nothing to do with creating the app,' she protested.

'Prove it,' pressed the woman.

'She don't need to prove nothing.'

Elena wheeled around to find the face of her saviour. It was Sasha, but Elena didn't recognise her right away. Her face was badly bruised, worse even than it had been after the incident in Marylebone.

'Me and her spent years together working the streets for Emerson Smith,' Sasha continued, matching the woman from the wall for ferocity. 'So don't talk to me about proof, yeah?'

The two women eyed one another for a moment, then the aggressor gave way. 'Well, read then!' she ordered.

Elena couldn't take her eyes off her friend. She wanted to embrace her, but now was not the time. Sasha smiled her encouragement. As Elena wrenched her gaze away, she realised that Sasha's appearance was not unique; cuts and bruises were everywhere. These women were refugees, escaped from the battlefront.

Eventually she managed to read on. 'The next point is: describe in detail any problems you've had with the app.'

Again a multitude of voices sounded, as each woman tried to out-shout the others. Instinctively, Elena seized control. 'If Pimple is listening, let's each be as clear as we possibly can be,' she said, measured and authoritative. 'We have a chance to change the way we work. Perhaps it's best if we speak in turns?'

Nobody moved at first. Then the woman in the blazer raised a hand. A number of the others scoffed. Rumour had it that some high-end, independent escorts – women who had never in their lives worked for pimps – were also signing up to Pimple. Here surely was one example. Elena gestured to her, realising she was waiting for an invitation to speak.

'Hello, I'm Caroline.' She gave a little wave. 'How do we deal with the problem of virgin clients?' Her voice was rather forced, overly nasal, particularly when saying the phrase 'virgin clients', as though she were hoping to claim credit for the term's invention. A few women tutted impatiently, but she was undeterred. 'What I mean is, it's all well and good when a client has a star rating of five or a star rating of one, based on a large number of reviews. But what about when a customer has no rating? Or a weaker rating, based on only one or two reviews? How do we protect ourselves against the risk of them being... rotten?'

'You mean the risk of them being a fucking psycho?' asked a short, wavy-haired woman with a fiery tone.

Again laughter circled and Caroline nodded sheepishly. People were reluctant to speak for a while after that. The call had been for problems, not for solutions. What more was there to say? Faces began to turn expectantly back towards Elena.

'Any other problems?' she asked.

'Hang on!' somebody shouted. 'That it? We not gonna talk about fixing it?'

'Pimple is listening, my friend,' said Sasha. 'Let them fix it.'

'I gotta problem,' said the woman from the wall. 'What are those girls doing 'ere? They don't come from where we come from. You ever worked the streets, girl?' She was brandishing a multi-ringed finger at Caroline, who looked around for help.

'No,' she began. 'I'm... I'm self-employed.'

Glossy brown hair fell only to her shoulders, and she was wearing a set of small gold earrings. She wore glasses, too. She was a natural target.

'So why the fuck you on Pimple?' asked the woman. 'Pimple's about fucking over the pimps. This ain't a game.' She had begun to prowl forwards.

'It can be anything to anyone,' Elena cut in. She couldn't help herself. 'It's ours. It belongs to all of us. We decide how to use it, when to use it, when not to. That's the point. It's there if we need it, whoever needs it. When you're done, you're done. That's the beauty of Pimple. Its control. That's why it's different to what came before.'

The woman arched as if to argue, but a ripple of murmured support made her think better of it. From that point, Elena's most unexpected hold over proceedings continued unbroken.

Discussion came from all four corners of the room, with Elena as the focal point. More questions about fees cropped up. Points about the legality of the app were raised. At one stage a curly-haired woman with an Irish accent talked about how she only wanted to use the app until she had made enough money to walk away from prostitution, prompting others to share longer-term plans of their own.

After a good hour's discussion, with no pause for breath, a skinny man with acne poked his head around the door to tell the women that they had to be out of the room in five minutes, because he had booked it for a meeting. The warning was met with a barrage of verbal abuse.

A sombre-faced woman then cut through the crowd of bodies – bodies that seemed more than willing to part for her. Her black skin was perfectly smooth. She was older than most of the women, but it was evident only in the aura of authority that surrounded her. Before she spoke she cast a look around the room, calling the women to order.

'Some of you know me,' she smiled. 'For those who don't, my name is Viola. I know girls of sixteen,' she paused. 'Who work in walk-ups, in parlours, in apartments. I hear about younger girls still.' Again she paused. 'How do we help them? Pimple's a start, but it can't stop here. How do we help the house girls? The parlour girls?'

There were mutterings around the room, but nobody seemed to want to voice their views openly. A few heads turned to Elena. She remained silent. More heads turned, willing her to speak.

'I share your concerns, Viola,' she eventually said. 'I've worked in the houses. No person should have to live that way. But I do not know how we help.' She spread out her hands. 'I don't have answers.'

The older woman surveyed her. Her eyes were a deep brown. She was almost sage-like. That such people could emerge from the darkness of the London sex trade filled Elena with hope.

'The app is not just better for us,' said Viola. 'It's better for everyone. It's better for the punters too. Many girls who manage to escape their pimps will quit the business in the blink of an eye, and I support that with a full heart. We all should strive for that. But for those of us who – for whatever reason – can't yet walk away, Pimple is the answer. We've got to force this whole thing online.' She had a stirring voice. The room hung on her every word. 'We have a window of opportunity. We have to take the fight to the very worst of the pimps – for all our friends who cannot break free. We have to free them.'

There was a chorus of approval, but then came the question: 'How?'

'We help the app. We spread the word. We persuade the whorehouse regular Joes to get online.'

'Pimps'll come for us, man,' said one woman, with a thick accent. 'They'll come for us, they'll kill us.'

'It's going to be a struggle,' Viola replied. 'Make no mistake. This is not going to be pretty. If you want out, you get out. Me? I'm done with fear. We have a chance to put the fear in them.' She rapped her knuckles on her chest. 'I'm taking it.'

A few women were silent, but most roared their support. It was at this moment that the spotty-faced man reappeared to inform them that their time was up.

Contact details were shared. Hands were slapped. Plans about how to disrupt the brothels and the red light zones would be posted on the online forums. There was talk of a second meeting, but it was then decided that co-ordination was best left to Pimple. The women began to drain from the room, slowly, reluctantly.

Elena and Sasha took the stairs together and, once out of sight, embraced.

'What happened, Sasha?' asked Elena.

'Smith locked it down after you left. But I figured this'd work,' she grinned weakly, gesturing at her injuries. 'Worked before, didn't it? Just had to get myself into a hospital and away from his boys. Then I ran.'

Sasha now lived nearby, in the rougher end of Shoreditch, where she slept under a bridge. Elena insisted that she come back to her flat at once. Sasha agreed, and the two women promised to have each other's back through whatever lay ahead. They talked about the future as they walked. They talked of possibility. They whispered of their fears.

11

The Knightsbridge Parlour

Emerson Smith paced along a quiet street in Knightsbridge. His croc-
odile leather burgundy-coloured boots sparkled in the lamplight. A
sharp heel click followed him. He wore a three-piece navy blue suit,
with a fine thin tie and a customarily garish watch. His beard was, as
ever, thick but well kept, and heavily perfumed.

The lines of high houses rose like stony sentinels on either side of
him – tasteful interplays between beige sandstone and sturdy crimson
brick. They stared each other down across the wide open road, each
equally formidable. Towards the end the residential rise tailed off, giving way to a crooked set of shops. One sold furniture of a plain but
trendy variety. Its window was sparsely decorated with a few carefully
placed stools and a low-slung coffee table. A mirror hung there also,
bordered by an intricate garland on which perched a flock of oaken
songbirds.

The succession of shops were much the same, though their wares
were vastly different. Next was a café where a black Americano
would set you back two pounds fifty. Then a gloomy restaurant, filled
with stately women who spoke through rhombus-shaped mouths, as
if hooked by stray fishing lures. A clear formula bound the shops
together.

Emerson stopped in front of an establishment that was true to the
same minimalist code. The building melted seamlessly into the shop
parade, distinguished only by a darker set of windows and no apparent
signage. The door was panelled like a flat black carapace. A gleam-
ing golden knocker dangled; underneath sat a similarly golden oblong
plaque bearing the engraving *The Knightsbridge Parlour*. These words

were discernible only from the last of the steps that led up to the heavy-set door.

Emerson steadied himself at the foot of the steps. He patted down his lapels, pressed a palm to his forehead and reflattened his plastered hair. He then marched up to the door and rapped twice upon the polished knocker.

A mountainous man in a tent-like suit pulled back the door with a look of instinctive distrust. Emerson met his suspicion with a calm and unyielding stare. No words passed between them. With a flick of a finger, the doorman bade him raise his arms. Emerson complied. The man fondled him from underarm to ankle. Each slap of the hand landed firm but in restrained fashion upon his torso and flanks. Satisfied, the man then gave way like the great door before him, ushering Emerson towards a reception desk.

A long, narrow hallway revealed itself, distinctively Victorian in style. The richly veined wood of a reception desk stood to his immediate left. Ahead a matching bannister wound its way upstairs. The hall was softly lit; frosty, translucent lampshades were suckered to the creamy wallpaper. Light music and chatter emanated from what seemed to be the entrance to a lounge, up ahead to the right.

A dainty woman – Ukrainian, by the look and sound of her – stood behind the desk. She smiled the kind of counterfeit, toothy grin that Emerson knew only too well. She wore a lacy but mostly unrevealing dress; fine jewellery hung from her like tinsel from a Christmas tree.

'Good evening, sir,' she chimed, as Emerson approached. 'Welcome to The Knightsbridge Parlour. Do you have a reservation?'

Emerson shook his head briskly.

'No problem,' she continued. 'Have you visited us before?'

He nodded. 'Excellent. Could I please take your name, sir?'

'Emerson,' he answered.

'Lovely, and your surname?'

'You won't be needing that.'

The woman, who had been operating on autopilot, appeared suddenly flushed. 'Sir, I'm afraid that I must insist…'

Emerson cut her off. 'You don't need it.'

He spoke irritably, and looked away as she floundered. In actuality he was quite calm, but he was enjoying her discomfort. *The customer is always right*, she would doubtless be thinking. The gormless door-man was no use to her now. Inevitably, she soon conceded.

'Not to worry then,' she stammered. 'Your card, sir.' She handed him a queen of hearts, which he duly snatched. 'First door on the right.' She gestured towards the gently humming room along the hallway. 'Enjoy your evening, sir.'

Emerson had set off before the sentence left her lips.

Entering the room was like walking into a densely statued tomb. Women of varying shapes and sizes were standing in clumps. These clustered mannequins seemed to be arranged by theme – primarily by race, but also by hair colour, and perhaps even by build. Every one of them followed a similar aesthetic, bedecked with semi-precious stones, fine and colourful feathers and neatly knotted ribbons.

There was flesh enough on show to arouse intrigue, but little enough to bolster the notion that the place was of high-end status. As if on cue, each woman turned to face Emerson as he entered, like meerkats alerted to a nearby lion.

A bar ran along one side of the square room, behind which lay all manner of spirits, housed by an armada of glass vessels that boasted a great deal more diversity than the assembled women.

Heavily cushioned furniture had been scattered around the room. Several of the women had already been siloed away to a velvety retreat. Their captors, suave and oily men, leaned forwards so that only their chosen counterpart might distinguish their murmurings. Those counterparts were all giggling dutifully. Between each couple, mostly lodged beneath a half-finished cocktail, lay a playing card of the house of hearts. Now a soggy afterthought, these cards were the unfading scars of transaction. Once handed to a woman, her services were as good as bought.

An obelisk-like creature, surely the brother of the burly specimen on the door, surveyed the scene from a shadowy corner. The amal-gamation of expensive smells, stock jazz music and dim lighting had given the place a false air of refinement. No doubt this softer form of shop window served to slacken the morality of prospective customers.

Emerson could not help but be impressed. He gazed around the room, soon locating his quarry. A woman shaped as if to disembark her stool, but Emerson strode right by her. Indeed, the strangely bold and bearded man bypassed each and every one of the subtly craning women, aiming instead for a scarcely perceptible corner door, emblazoned simply with the word *Private*. The slumbering overseer stirred, but could not raise his hulking form in time to prevent Emerson from slipping through it and out of sight.

What confronted him was a capriciously furnished study. A tan-skinned man sat behind a chestnut desk. A Turkish rug was draped across the floor between them. A distinctly Tudor-looking bookcase was nudged up against one wall, bearing a smorgasbord of odds and ends, including ancient and impractical forms of weaponry, but few books.

The person behind the desk was Bledi Shala – arguably the lead man in a loosely correlated syndicate of London-based Albanian pimps. He was bald, and his skin had a sempiternal sheen, like the surface of a thickly algaed pond. He was also a man whom Emerson knew a great deal about.

Shala had been born to a poor family in the outskirts of Tirana in the 1970s. His interests had led him inexorably into the local police force and his character had soon corrupted him. In the run-up to the Kosovo War he had helped to facilitate the smuggling of arms to the Kosovo Liberation Army – not through any unity of purpose, but purely for the promise of gain. But he soon discovered a more lucrative niche.

In the face of Serbian persecution in the late 1990s – a wave of terror comprised of murder, torture, rape and arson – Kosovar Albanians began to stream across the Albanian border in search of refuge. Bledi Shala had laid himself down upon that border like a bulbous, open-jawed snake. Scores of women and children, displaced and frenzied, fled unwittingly into his gullet. He made them promises of security, of stability, even of prosperity – while always thinking only of his own.

With the help of several cousins who were already operating in the United Kingdom, he acquired a dysfunctional and dilapidated massage parlour in central London. He then regurgitated his crop of refugees and had soon set them to slavery. The business model proved successful. After a few short years he commanded a small empire of parlours and brothels, all fuelled by the conflict in the Balkans and its resulting fallout.

He snapped straight as Emerson entered the room. His eyes were darting and humourless, like the eyes of a roving hawk. Emerson marched directly to the desk and placed the queen of hearts upon the tabletop's soft padding.

'We need to talk,' he said, with a singularity of purpose that could not be ignored. Great club-like hands then came tumbling through the fragrant air, landing on Emerson's shoulders and jerking him backwards. The ponderous guardsman had arrived. But Bledi waved him off with a listless flick of his hand, and the stony man recoiled sheepishly. Emerson patted down his lapels.

'A most unexpected pleasure, Mr Smith. Please do sit.'

His voice was gravelly and harsh – a voice ill-suited to pleasantries. Still, Emerson accepted the invitation to sit and placed a hand on each knee. For a short while the men absorbed one another in silence. A chain dangled from Bledi's neck – a lengthy, interlocking line of tiny platinum ovals. It lay on a bed of dense chest hair, visible between the three-button divide of his shirt.

'May I offer you a drink?'

'No, thank you,' answered Emerson, his gaze unswerving.

'How may I be of service, Mr Smith?' asked Bledi, unclasping his hands theatrically.

'I am not one for mincing words, Mr Shala.'

'Nor I,' came the quick reply. 'And please, call me Bledi.'

'I'll mince none today. I've come to speak to you about a grave threat to our businesses. Are you familiar with the mobile app Pimple?'

'I am,' answered Bledi in a measured tone. A corner of his stubble-bordered lips curled. 'And I am acutely familiar with the threat it poses to *your* business.'

Emerson, outwardly unflappable, saw this as an early bid for the high ground. Again he palmed his hair flat, for the first time breaking eye contact with his adversary.

'My business, your business. It's all the same.'

'Not so,' said Bledi, flatly. 'It strikes me that those with girls out on the roads will bear the brunt of this Pimple. My girls work under lock and key, as well you know.'

'You misunderstand.'

'How so?' enquired Bledi.

'You are quite correct that I, and others like me, bear the greater short-term risk, due chiefly to my distribution channels. But you've seen only one side of the coin. You've not felt the pressure yet because for now it's the sellers – the women – who are driving the growth of the app. But the network will spread like wildfire if left unchecked. The flow of demand will shift. The punters will become the instigators. And then, when it is already too late, your bars and parlours will start to dry up.'

'Nonsense!' bellowed the stout Albanian, eyeballs popping, his sleek persona shattered. He was on his feet. His fist closed upon the desk.

Emerson rose to meet him. 'I know you to be a man of business, Mr Shala,' he continued. 'I cannot say the same for all your compatriots. That is why I came to you.'

Bledi rounded the table to confront Emerson. He bared a set of yellowing teeth and hissed a rebuttal. 'You know what I see, Emerson Smith? Desperation. I see it all slipping away.' He made a theatrical gesture. 'Sand between your fingers.'

Emerson did not flinch. He leaned in a little closer. 'Mark my words,' he breathed. 'It will take a co-ordinated effort to beat this thing. You have my number. Call me when you start to feel the squeeze.'

'There will be no squeeze,' rasped Bledi. Still they stood at close quarters, like prize-fighters at weigh-in. 'I must now ask you to leave, Mr Smith.'

The tension held a little longer. Then Emerson smiled a wry smile and took a small step backwards. 'I hope to see you again soon, Mr Shala,' he said, extending a steady palm.

Bledi shook his hand, but with no great gusto. 'Arda,' he said. 'Please show Mr Smith out.'

One of the two great-framed guardians was holding the door open; the strains of a saxophone drifted in.

Emerson turned to depart, but doubled back for one final note of warning. 'The tide will turn, Mr Shala, whether we like it or not. We can either turn with it, or be washed away.'

Bledi's eyes blazed with fury. He turned his back, and the watchman led Emerson out of the room. All eyes were on him once more as he passed through the sordid selection chamber. His mind busily digesting the encounter, he returned none of the glances. Had he scare-mongered sufficiently? To what extent did Bledi buy his own bluster? He would be a crucial cog in the resistance, that much was certain: the lynchpin of the Albanian whorehouses, and the key to onboarding their various masters.

Emerson had soon been bundled out of the front door. He straightened out his suit and sauntered along the quiet road, past the obsessively trimmed hedgerows. He whistled a tune to himself, feeling faintly satisfied. He did not expect to hear from his Albanian counterpart any time soon; but he was convinced the groundwork would pay off, whenever the pressure began to tell. He had always considered himself a keen opportunist, which – coupled with a certain litheness of principle and a penchant for ruthlessness – had allowed him to rise from the muck of his upbringing to a level of prominence. His opportunism and his restlessness fed off of one another; his desires were insatiable.

As a younger man – already risen from destitution – he had peddled all manner of contraband, flitting between substances as consumer demand shifted, and ultimately weaving his way to the bartering of flesh. He considered himself wholly distinct from all others in his trade, given as he was to the most extreme form of narcissism. But there could be no denying that he was sharp, and while the rise of Pimple had already caused him significant distress, he had also sensed in it the aroma of opportunity.

As Emerson walked, he began taking notes on his phone. He noted down the address of The Knightsbridge Parlour. He noted down the entry procedure, down to the very words he had exchanged with the receptionist. He made note of the number and respective statures of the security staff. He sketched out the layout of the building, such as he understood it, labelling each section according to its function, and made a point of underlining the words 'Shala's study'.

For all Pimple had taken from Smith, it had given him something too: the pretext to parlay with his fellow pimps. Pimps in London – particularly pimps who were the equal of Emerson Smith – were understandably hostile creatures. But with Pimple as a cover, Emerson had licence to roam. Bledi Shala was not unique in dismissing him, and many a guileless pimp would do the same over the coming months. And while they laughed, Emerson continued his meticulous documentation of their affairs: the chief surveyor in a sweeping, undercover census.

After all, if the events of the moment had proven anything, it was that information was king, and Emerson Smith well knew it.

12

UX

Annie's mind was alive with possibility. All that she passed, she pondered. She muttered the occasional word of condemnation beneath her breath, alternating between 'relic' and 'dinosaur'. Nothing was safe from her piercing blue eyes. She was in triumphant spirit. To once again be at the centre of – nay, conducting! – a tectonic shift in the way that human beings interact was to her the sweetest form of inebriation.

She sauntered smugly by an idle row of black cabs that were queuing up outside a Tube stop. Arms sagged over window frames. Craggy faces leered begrudgingly from within. A few wore flat caps, perhaps to accentuate that old-school charm that the advertisements adorning their doors so frequently alluded to. *Take a ride in London's iconic black cab!* read one door. Annie scoffed. How absurd it was, the idea of a thing highlighting its own antiquity in an attempt to draw in customers.

'Sounding your own death knell,' she muttered, before deciding that it had in fact tolled long ago.

Later she stood in a queue for coffee, the electric blue of her eyes still roaming. The very concept of a queue was un-modern, she decided, as she inched towards the counter. She stood imperiously among the droopy bodies and allowed her mind to wander, conjuring grand designs. She unpackaged the queue into its component parts, into people – in this instance, people made flaccid by the earliness of the hour. She pried into their brains: why were they in the queue? Why were they willing to queue? What might they be doing otherwise? How might she help them?

Aha! She had it: an app that allows customers to participate in a queue remotely. Venues would cater to their customers not in the order in which they arrived, but according to the order of an online waiting list. Customers could therefore turn up at the very moment that their digital selves were arriving at the top of the pecking order, freeing up the time they would have otherwise spent standing in line. It was a good idea; she was enthused. But before she could burrow further into it, she arrived, in somewhat timely fashion, at the front of the queue.

She flowed along the gum-gripped pavement, coffee holders in hand, hair flouncing in the wind. As she strolled, she passed by another half-dozen broken businesses – a myriad of matchmakers, dwindling in practical value. She was unwittingly alert to such things at present, just as one discovers a thing only for everyday encounters with that thing to suddenly multiply.

She passed by an estate agents, all block colours and invitingly luminescent. There were hollowed-out orbs for seats, dangling like anglerfish antennae. The tables and desks lacked clean-cut edges; everything had a sort of fibreglass lustre. It was a valiant attempt to imply modernity through design, but ultimately a failed one.

She arrived outside a peculiar box-shaped building. Multicoloured balconies protruded at random from the grey exterior. The whole thing looked as though it could have sprung up from the concrete that very morning. Annie entered and climbed a number of floors by foot. She soon stood before flat number 712 and rapped sharply on the door.

'Oh Peter!' she crooned.

Veronica opened the door and shushed her reproachfully. Annie cackled as she was dragged inside, struggling to keep the coffees balanced.

'Will you hush, woman?' hissed Veronica.

'Come on,' said Annie. 'Loosen up.'

'I do not feel loose, Annie. I do not feel loose.' Veronica was clenching her fists, gripping in them the ends of her sleeves. 'This whole thing is moving too fast. User numbers are ballooning, men more quickly than the women...'

'Glorious!' interrupted Annie, setting the coffees down upon the table – one in front of a tired-looking Peter Froome, who was poring over a laptop, and who waved her a sleepy hello. 'That'll kick rates up.'

'Annie, all this money, the server space, the processing power: it's all growing and it's growing too fast. You can't just sweep away a footprint this big.'

'We've managed so far.'

'*We've* managed,' snapped Veronica. 'Peter and I. You don't have to worry about this sort of stuff. You just assume it's in hand. We need to talk about how to manage this, Annie.'

'Manage it?' said Annie, eyes widening. The panda-faced Peter became wholly absorbed with his laptop. 'It's not ours to manage, Veronica. It's their revolution. We are but humble facilitators.'

'There won't be a revolution if we're caught out.'

'Ron!' cried Annie, exasperated. 'May I please just drink my coffee in peace? We'll talk through all of this. I promise. We have the whole day ahead of us.'

'Fine,' said Veronica, wheeling away swiftly and planting herself down at the table.

The space around them was sparsely furnished. Daylight streamed in from high, oblong windows. Several squat servers stood in a row against one wall, humming an uneven tune. A mass of cables flowed between them. The lengthy table carried a number of monitor screens of varying sizes. The room purred with the sound of digital activity.

It belonged to Peter, who had inherited it from his parents. He had been renting it out to the same tenants for years – a couple who had got engaged long ago, only to become trapped in the purgatory between engagement and marriage. The wedding had finally taken place a few months back, coinciding with a move away from the city. Peter had been slow to replace them.

When the Pimple app was conceived, it had been hosted on Veronica's personal server, but a more scalable solution was soon required. When Peter mentioned the flat, Annie had urged Veronica to pose the question. It was perfect. Peter had buckled instantly. Servers had been upgraded. Infrastructure, both physical and digital, had been installed. Capillary by capillary, the capacious box had become the beating heart of the network.

Peter had been rather swept up by the whole affair, having waded in initially out of affection for Veronica. He was from an exceptionally wealthy family whom he mostly despised, but put up with. In his late twenties he had become the chief technology officer of Millennial Credit. For Annie and Veronica he had always shown the utmost admiration, in his own quiet way. In the case of Veronica, that admiration had morphed over time into adoration, or so Annie had always believed. His love for her friend was, to Annie's mind, of the unspoken but obvious kind. He was too meek a man for grand gestures and Veronica appeared unconcerned by such frivolity, superficially at least. And so their feelings existed as a richly coloured reef beneath a clouded sea, discernible but faint.

'How did it go?' asked Veronica.

Annie took a long sip of coffee. 'Extremely well.'

Veronica, increasingly agitated, waited for her to expound further upon the user meeting, but to no avail. When Annie finally spoke it was to utter a question.

'What is the limit of evolution, I wonder?'

'Oh God,' seethed Veronica. 'Annie…'

'What I mean is, is there a point at which a species hits its evolutionary apex – and can adapt no further?'

'Of course not,' came the unexpected voice of Peter. Veronica shot him a furious look.

'Oh?' Annie retorted at once. 'So the ape – left unchecked – will one day reach a human-like level of cerebral development?'

'Quite possibly.'

'And the mongoose, too? And the starfish and the shrew?'

Peter looked either a little stuck, or more than a little wearied. The greater expertise in such matters was clearly his, but Annie – a keen sophist – didn't regard knowledge as a prerequisite for vehemence.

Veronica was drawn in. 'Intelligence is not at the summit of all evolutionary paths,' she said tersely. 'The starfish might simply get stickier and stickier. Why does a starfish need intelligence, anyway?'

Annie cocked her head, considering.

'Can we please talk about this goddamn app?' demanded Veronica, her patience finally snapping.

'OK, Ron. I'm sorry,' Annie conceded. 'Talk to me.'

Thus ensued a long and arduous conversation that centred on Veronica's gripes – technical and ethical. She looked increasingly frustrated as the discussion rolled on. When it came to the minutiae of running an enterprise, Annie's way was always the path of least resistance; Veronica would often protest that her solutions to problems were unsatisfactorily vague.

Veronica pointed out that the meeting point function was not running as smoothly as it might be. Users were frequently befuddled when buildings were pinpointed, but not a flat number, or a road was indicated without making plain the fact that one party would be arriving by car and would not be getting out of it.

'Can't we simply attach some kind of explanatory note?' asked Annie.

'Well, yes. Maybe. But I also thought that categorising meet points might make sense. By car, in flat, on road, and so on,' said Veronica.

'Excellent idea, Veronica. Let's go with both,' said Annie. And that, for her, was the end of the matter.

'So let's map out the user experience now,' persisted Veronica.

'Haven't we just done that? Locations now come categorised, with note functionality if necessary.'

'Well, we've suggested that as a potential solution, yes,' answered Veronica. 'But we need much more information to implement it. At what point will the customer be asked to categorise? Will it be mandatory? How will these new features look? Where will the note sit? Can we write this into the code easily?'

'Oh Veronica, the two of you are much better at that sort of stuff than me!' cried Annie. 'I trust you.'

Veronica turned an alarming shade of red. 'And what exactly will you be doing in the meantime?'

Annie's usual answer to this kind of jibe was that she ran the marketing – which in so small an organisation encapsulated everything from customer acquisition to brand, promotion, and so on. The most recent of these initiatives had revolved around a play on words, one

Annie was particularly proud of. Free journeys were routinely offered to first-time users of the taxi app Uber as a means of coaxing them into trialling the service. The company itself bore the cost of these promotions as the drivers still needed to be paid. It was the same with Pimple, right down to the wording: debutant punters were offered a 'free ride' the first time they used the app. It had gone down a storm, and the vendors were none the wiser.

The conversation surged back and forth over a great many additional points: pricing squabbles between users, and Pimple's involvement (or lack of involvement) in settling such disagreements; whether or not a reserve fund, fed by facilitation fee money, ought to be established to reimburse aggrieved customers; whether or not the social scoring system was powerful enough – as an indicator of trustworthiness – to preclude Pimple from ever needing to mediate in disputes. Peter rarely intervened.

'Most of all,' said Veronica finally, 'I am increasingly uneasy about the spread of rates being charged across the user base. It's too wide. Far too wide. It's wrong, Annie. It's cancerous.'

Veronica had identified that an elite band of app users had developed so loyal a customer base, and so stellar a Pimple score, that they were able to charge rates that were verging on the ludicrous, especially in relation to those charged by women at the opposite end of the spectrum. Inevitably, attractiveness and sexuality were the crucial factors in a user's pricing power.

'I think we need to consider a maximum rate cap,' declared Veronica. 'To go alongside the minimum rate rule.'

Annie baulked at the suggestion. 'You're suggesting that we limit the horizons of these women? Who on earth are we to do that, Veronica? Why are we even doing this if not to empower people – to get them earning more money?'

'I'm uncomfortable with the idea of one person earning exponentially more than another for doing the same damn thing,' said Veronica.

'It's a sad state of affairs, Ron, but that's just a reality of business, and of life! Some people are better at business than others, and those people get paid more. At least they're all now equal in not losing out to the middleman. We mustn't intervene.'

'I disagree. I believe we ought to.' Veronica's slender eyebrows were tilted inwards like a burdened tightrope.

'It's not our place to. Don't you see? It's not our movement. It's theirs,' said Annie, with an air of finality.

The argument reared its head again later that same day, when Annie gave her account of the recent Pimple meeting. Veronica suggested that they ought to somehow pour cold water on the women's plans to go after the massage parlour regulars.

'We're moving too quickly, too quickly,' she murmured. 'These are violent men, Annie.'

'That's why we're here, Veronica!' exclaimed Annie. She found her friend's position hard to fathom. 'What is it you're suggesting? That we leave them alone? Let them be? Because they're so very wicked, so violent?'

The disagreements persisted, wearying and futile, for weeks; eventually, the women ground each other down to a sullen impasse. Veronica stopped pestering, but she also withdrew her enthusiasm for the project. Instead she had the air of one working to fulfil a solemn duty.

Meanwhile, Annie held an ace up her sleeve. She laid plans to use the Pimple app as if she were a genuine user, in the hope of quieting some of Veronica's doubts through first-hand experience. But each time she came to the moment of truth, she backed out. In two weeks she reneged on four such arrangements, earning herself a volley of poor reviews.

She would redouble her efforts. She could not afford to lose Veronica.

13

Misgivings

Warren lurked in wait on a quiet Soho side street. The nights were beginning to warm, and dark had not yet fallen. A reeking mass of human flesh went chugging past his unmarked car, skin jostling like a gelatinous dessert; as he passed, he drained the last of a deeply ironic energy drink before slinging the empty can to the ground. Warren was irked. His head tilted in a kind of shivering motion. Stowing his flask along with his thoughts, he stepped out of the car into the street.

The odour of the passing behemoth lagged behind him in the way that exhaust fumes flutter behind a truck. Warren sniffed violently, drawing the attentions of the man, who turned around and headed back towards Warren. Warren stood waiting, chin a little raised, surveying the approach through narrowed eyes. He bore none of the identifying marks of a policeman.

'You got a problem? You ill?' The looming load coughed. The words sounded as though they were struggling to escape his gullet, and his face gave the impression of implosion – its outermost parts infringing further and further upon his features.

'I do.' So frank was Warren's admission that the man slowed. 'I'm going to have to ask you to pick up that can.'

The man's skin rippled unnaturally. 'You fuckin' crazy, son.' He jabbed a flabby finger-end against his own lightly tanned temple.

Warren looked on in bemusement. 'Not crazy, no. Upset that you've so little regard for this fine city.'

'You crazy!' repeated the man, close enough now to swing for Warren, but clearly hoping – as animals hope in the wild – that a show of force would be sufficient to cause his adversary to scarper.

No such luck. They were now squaring up. Warren, tall and burly enough, was by some way dwarfed. The tension built. The trembling-lipped litterbug, unnerved by Warren's stillness, shuffled closer. He seemed momentarily at a loss, then swung a pudgy, thunderous fist from waist height on a slow upward trajectory, as if through treacle, aiming for Warren's head: a trebuchet taking aim at a sparrow.

Warren, in a sudden burst of litheness, evaded the oncoming arm and in a flash had a hold of its trailing counterpart. He folded the lagging arm up into the man's flabby back, and pressed him violently against the parked vehicle.

'What the fuck, man? What the fuck!' protested the man, his face pressed flat against the car window.

'I don't want to have tell you I'm a copper to make you do it,' breathed Warren. 'I just want you to do it. I'm going to let you go, and you're going to pick the can up, and you're going to find a home for it. Do you understand me?'

There was a pause while the man, still squashed against the car, considered his options. 'OK,' he said, rather timidly. 'Just let me go, man.'

Warren obliged and stepped back, holding his hands at his sides as if he'd performed a magic trick. The man, clearly embarrassed, shook himself off and darted – as best as he could dart – to the can's resting place. He swiped the thing up begrudgingly and began to rumble on down the road without uttering another word. Warren watched him go, catching his eye when he chanced a backward glance. When the man had disappeared, Warren followed in the same direction.

His footsteps echoed cleanly in the urban gorge. To his left, the stony bank of buildings suddenly gave way to a lower-walled courtyard. The space had a single door of rusted iron. Its exterior was crowned with a tier of tightly drawn cords, strung like the spine of a violin, which Warren perceived to be electrified. These wires, however, ran for only two-thirds of the length of wall, leaving a sizeable gap between their tail-ends and the resurgent high rise. Warren pondered briefly upon the strangeness of the fixing, and further upon the closeness of the futile and the incomplete.

He walked to the end of the alleyway and out onto a brightly lit lane. He turned left, passed a pair of bustling bars, and walked beneath the overhang of a theatre balcony. Frivolity filled the air. He consulted his phone to make sure he was on course. Sure enough, the agreed-to meeting place was just a few strides ahead.

Several weeks before, frustrated by the seemingly impenetrable veil surrounding Pimple and its creators, Warren had taken to the streets in search of answers. He had interviewed a number of low-star recruits by posing as a willing client. They were typically one- or two-star users, because that was all that Warren and his limited review history seemed capable of connecting with. Once or twice he'd interviewed a three-star, but the conversations were not entirely different; only the location and the assuredness of the woman seemed to change.

These conversations had brought the detective no closer to uncovering the mystery of the app's creators. Mostly the women seemed truly to know nothing of the architects of the platform. In a few cases they had picked up on whispers, but for the most part they neither knew nor cared about where the app had come from.

But ignorance was not the only barrier. Several of the women had put up a fierce defence of the app, refusing to say a word to Warren once he had revealed his true identity as a law enforcer. Their ferocity reminded him of that same, counter-intuitive zeal that had for years spurred on Sasha and other women like her to keep safe the secrets of their pimps. But with Pimple it was different. It was somehow more primal, more instinctive – driven by something deeper than fear. And who was there to fear anyway? That was the very problem.

Warren's phone buzzed. A notification from Pimple told him that he had arrived at the agreed-to location. He had been lost in thought. Arching up before him was a tall, narrow building. At its roots there was a softly glowing atrium, with a silver roller ripe for luggage standing by, but no cargo and no conductor. People were prancing in and out in great numbers.

Warren looked for a woman with red shoes, as he had been instructed. And there she was, seated on a low black pouffe. She had a great bush of seemingly irrevocably tangled hair, and she raised her eyebrows invitingly as she caught sight of him. Her eyes were intensely blue. Warren strode over to greet her.

'You must be Annie,' he said with a grin, stooping and extending his elbow.

'I must,' she replied. 'Lovely to meet you.'

'And you,' replied the detective.

She took his arm and they stood, wandering lazily in the direction of the lifts.

'Do you care for a drink first?' asked the woman. Warren was a little shocked, not just by the question but also by the phrasing; this was not the standard-issue vocabulary of a one-star user.

'Do I care for a drink?' he repeated. He noticed a busy bar area just ahead of the lifts. 'Yes. Why not?'

She smiled a toothy smile in reply, and together they passed into the bar. Once there, Warren ordered himself a beer.

'What would you like?' he asked, instantly wondering why on earth he had offered.

'How very generous!' she replied. 'I'll have a glass of red wine, if that's OK? The best they have.'

'And will that be baked into the cost of this transaction?' asked Warren.

'Can be.' She smiled. 'Just tell me the price and I'll raise my rates accordingly.'

Warren laughed. He couldn't help it. The joke was more than unusual; it was enthralling.

He ordered the most expensive red that was available by the glass and together they floated towards a shadowy corner; they cleared away a few discarded glasses to make space for their own. Warren studied her face – which was dense with freckles – with great curiosity. Again he became lost in his thoughts.

'Tired?' she asked, snapping him back. She spoke with a thick Northern Irish accent, and he couldn't understand her at first above the noise of the bar. 'Busy day, was it?'

'Busy. Yes. Very busy. I suppose yours is just beginning.'

'Quite,' she replied. 'Does that disturb you?'

'No, not at all. Why would it?'

'Well, the thought of me with man after man after man. It's enough to disturb some men.'

'But not enough to put them off altogether,' said Warren, brusquely.

She smiled. 'No, rarely enough for that.'

Warren laughed contemptuously and turned his head to one side.

'How many jobs will you do in one night?' he asked, after a short pause.

'Could be as many as five or six, depending on the night. Why do you ask? You thinking of signing up? I had heard there were a few male workers on the app.'

'Depends,' he replied. 'What are the rates like?' Here Warren was feigning ignorance; he was now acutely familiar with the processes of the Pimple app.

'The rates? Well, you set your own rates, of course.'

'Yours seem rather expensive,' said Warren. 'For a one-star recruit, I mean.'

'Ha!' She laughed, taking a sip from her wine. 'I'm a bargain, I'll have you know.'

'And what is a bargain?'

'Getting more than you pay for.' There was a twinkle in her eye as she said the words, and she wriggled closer to the detective.

He felt suddenly uncomfortable, and clenched the knuckles of his left hand, then the knuckles of the right, twice, then the left again – all too quickly for her to have noticed. 'There's something about you, isn't there? You're no ordinary one-star.'

'Am I not?' she replied, now twiddling a strand of her hair with the fingers of her free hand. 'So what if I'm not?'

'Is that a confession?' he asked, leaning in menacingly. They held a quivering stare for several drawn-out seconds before he pulled back. 'You see, it matters a great deal if you are, indeed, extraordinary... I've come to realise that Pimple – it's a puzzle. But sadly there are far, far too many pieces. I could never hope to finish it, I think I'd go mad. No. What I'm looking for instead is the missing the piece, the outlier. The link in the chain that doesn't quite belong.'

'And why might you be looking for that, pray tell?' she asked.

'Why indeed.' Now the glint had passed to Warren's eye.

At this point the woman straightened, as if suddenly realising a terrible mistake in a game of chess that she had imagined she was winning. She looked lost for words, and drank again from her glass.

'Shall we head upstairs?' asked Warren, keen to press his advantage, whatever it meant.

'Yes. Let's.'

She gulped down her wine and they stood together. He took her by the hand and led her from the bar. No words were spoken as they waited for a lift to descend.

Then Warren spun to face her. 'And if I want to go again, so to speak, what then?' The woman's face was flushed. 'I mean, after the first time. Is there an extra cost for a second turn?'

She didn't answer for a moment. She seemed to be studying him. A soft note sounded as the lift landed.

'Oh yes. That's overtime, I'm afraid,' she said. 'Although having said that, it's very much a question of stamina. If you can fit a few rounds into your allotted time, then by all means, knock yourself out!'

Her manner seemed to have reverted. They entered the lift alongside several other people. She cosied up to his arm and laid her head on his broad shoulder. She smelled of tropical fruits. Warren stood stiffly, unsure of himself. If there was anything to crack, it had to be cracked quickly. They left the lift at floor nine, and the woman guided him softly towards her room. Their arms were still entwined, and she was squeezing each of his fingers. It seemed that all the time in the world was hers.

She unlocked a door using an access card from her purse. Beyond was a bed covered in orange flower petals. Empty glasses stood by. There was a view out across the darkened city. The tell-tale signs were all there.

She turned to face him at the doorway, and hooked a hand under each of his lapels. As though leading a beast of some kind, she steered him in and towards the bed, kicking the door closed. Her head and body swayed as she backed up, like a snake-charmer. Warren couldn't decide if it was a skilled or awkward retreat. There was so much to wonder about with this woman, but no more time to do it in.

'I'm sorry,' he said, as her legs struck the edge of the bed. 'I can't.'

She continued to cling to his coat, looking him over with great intensity. He held up his big left hand and pointed to a wedding ring with the other. Was it relief that then shone beyond her galaxy of freckles? She gave him no chance to decide, reeling him in closer as if to collapse him onto the bed on top of her. It was a blatant refusal to acknowledge the get-out-of-jail-free card, if that was what it was to her. Warren later wondered if the reeling in was a masterstroke: assassin to his suspicion.

'I really can't,' he said, pushing her away and onto the bed, alone.

She gazed up at him, looking both saddened and confused.

'I'm sorry,' he said again. Then he turned and hurriedly strode away.

He was in a trance-like state when he arrived back at the station. He went straight to the bathroom and splashed water on his face, looking at himself curiously in the mirror as it trickled from his eyes and into the sink.

No sooner had he entered his office upstairs than David Duffin was on him, ferreting this way and that, enquiring excitedly about progress – morphing into a vision of dejection on hearing that there was none.

Warren slumped into a chair between the desks of David and Grace. The three of them had spent months gathering intelligence on Pimple. Duffin had taken to the Pimple case with surprising alacrity. Ordinarily, he favoured bobbing along in the wake of a greater driving force, but not so with Pimple. Indeed, it was the suction provided by Duffin's enthusiasm that had galvanised his boss into action in the first place.

As the unit with perhaps the most hands-on experience of policing London's sex trade – which continued to flourish notwithstanding – the Pimple problem had inevitably wound its way to the desk of DCI Warren Beckett. At first, he had been somewhat loath to embark on an investigation that he had deemed – against the backdrop of the city's most egregious pimping rackets – an irrelevance. It was only the dogged interest and chivvying of Duffin that kept the case alive; even if it was, for a time, on life support. But the more he whittled away at his boss, the more the burly detective began to wake up to the subversive potential stored within the app.

Within a few short weeks, Duffin had won out; an investigation was in full swing. Ever since, Duffin had been trawling the online messaging boards for even the faintest glimmer of progress. It was he who had discovered the Pimple assemblies, and he who had mooted sending in their colleague Grace undercover.

And all the while, Pimple's incident reports continued to crop up. A theft in Camden. Battery in Battersea. It was as though the app's creators were teasing them.

Warren's empty-handed return weighed heavy upon the group. The avenues of exploration that were open to them had all come to a dead end. Where to next? Warren was unsure.

'Snap to it, chaps!' said Grace. 'I have news.'

She was a quirky sort of woman. If she had been allowed to she would have worn a streak of colour in her hair, but the superintendent had forbidden it. Her eyes were most unusual, a lifeless kind of green that bordered on yellow. She was boyish in physique, and carried herself in a boyish way too, and yet was by no means unattractive. On more than one occasion she had had to bat away the advances of male colleagues, and she spared no thought for their feelings when batting. She had a lively, Northern accent.

'I, being the wonder that I am, may be onto something,' she announced.

'What?' demanded Warren and David in unison.

'I'll come onto that, but before I do, allow me to educate you as to how Pimple works. As you know, the app charges users a facilitation fee of two per cent, which is carved out of every transaction. And as you also know, we have a pair of working accounts on Pimple. Boss' – here she was addressing Warren – 'I've taken the liberty of hijacking your account. Hope you don't mind. Yesterday, your account engaged mine in a twenty-minute contract, priced at two hundred pounds. Keep it together, Duffin.'

Needless to say, David had been one of the men who had tried for her affections. He now blushed.

'I was able to attach a trace program to the funds as they left your account,' she continued.

'Grace!' David clapped his hands.

'Hold your horses. I haven't reached the complicated part yet,' said Grace. 'The bulk of the money runs directly into my bank account. They seem to have developed a bespoke payments platform, or else they've repurposed some existing infrastructure. The facilitation fee appears to land in some kind of digital wallet.'

Both men strained to follow all this; neither knew much about payment technologies. Certainly they knew nothing about digital wallets.

'Can we tell who it belongs to?' asked Warren.

'No,' said Grace. 'But the money can't just stay in there. It's a lot like a real wallet. Useful for short-term storage, but with limited space, and limited security.'

'So what becomes of it?' asked David.

Grace smiled. 'They sell the money via a platform called DCX. It's a digital currency exchange.'

Warren exchanged glances with David; again, baffled.

'You know. Like Bitcoin?' continued Grace.

'I've heard of it,' offered David.

Grace shook her head despairingly. 'Here's what you need to know. It's an exchange for currencies that are online and decentralised – in other words, there's a finite amount of each one and the central banks have no say in their value. It's totally off the grid, basically.'

'So…' began Warren. 'So… we lose the money in this exchange?'

'Precisely. They likely convert it back into sterling later on, but by that time, we're lost.'

There was another pause.

'You'll forgive me for not lighting the fireworks,' said Warren.

'Well!' answered Grace. 'It's a start, isn't it?'

'May I make a suggestion?' said David.

'Please,' said Warren.

'I think we ought to talk to the administrator of this currency platform. They might be able to help.' David turned to Grace. 'Assuming they're not also shrouded in mystery?'

'No,' she replied, seemingly still wounded by Warren's lack of enthusiasm. 'They'll be contactable I'm sure. DCX is pretty well known. Has some big-name backers.'

'Let's get a name and bring them in for a chat,' said Warren. 'Grace, exceptional work.'

The trio instantly set about contacting the network. For the first time since the start of the investigation, it felt like genuine progress was at hand.

PART III

Restoration

14

The Founding of the Fist

The men were seated around a rectangular table in a softly lit room, high up on the 39th floor of a City skyscraper. Two connecting sides of the space were windows, offering broad views of London right out to where the concrete thins. The building itself looked like a pinstriped cigarette, one that had been poorly rolled and unsatisfactorily smoked.

They were in the swankiest function room of one of those lofty London restaurant bars that fuel the constant demands of corporate bellies in the working week. Brokers, lawyers and bankers: they all came and invariably fought for their right to pick up the bill. On this particular evening the room was host to a different breed. More or less every major pimp in London was present.

Bledi Shala was among them, surrounded by a handful of his swarthy associates. There were more than a few family ties between them, with Bledi acting as the undisputed patriarch. There was an informal faction of south London pimps, who had gravitated towards one another, not knowing what else to do. They wore pronounced scowls and, with the exception of one man, Reed McCoy, they looked physically intimidating; but ironically, it was Reed who was being given the widest berth. He hadn't yet said anything. He seemed not to even have looked at anyone, and yet he never seemed to blink. He was totally bald and simply dressed. His black, buffed skin was entirely unblemished. McCoy was said to be prone to maniacal outbursts of violence; he was the sort of man who was trailed by a host of wild and often grossly exaggerated tales. The fact that his name was so Irish-sounding somehow added to his mystique. The pimps from south London were for the most part embittered rivals. Their clientele tended not to be as affluent as the average punter in west or central London, which made for intensified competition.

There was also a smattering of solitary characters, mostly hailing from the more benevolent end of the sex trade spectrum. They operated near-equitable partnerships with their female associates. A good many of them had come in from London's commuter towns. One of these characters, John Spark, was seated at the corner of the table, looking fidgety. He was wearing a tatty old shirt; his hair fell in half-curled clumps around his face. He gave the impression of a run-down old hound. He ran a notoriously cheap bar and brothel in Putney, with just a handful of decaying bedrooms and himself as clerk.

Men like Spark, whose shabbily conducted affairs felt laughably innocuous when set against the exploits of London's worst pimps, were nonetheless seeing themselves eroded by the rise of the Pimple app. Any pimp was welcome at the table; there were common interests to defend. They had bunched up as impala do when threatened and, like impala, a few of them would soon make a show of their vitality – prancing and leaping about amid the quivering herd.

A fork chimed against a glass. Emerson Smith had been languidly surveying the scene with jutted jawline, perceptible even through his thick and oiled beard. He was wearing a purplish suit that blended in with the room. 'Skinny' Summers and Benz were seated on either side of him; John Canty was posted outside the room.

Smith rose to his feet, still chiming his fork; silence had not yet swept the room. Smith dropped the fork and smashed the glass against the table rim, effecting a shocked and sudden quiet. There was a pause, in which many hands twitched towards pockets. Smith then laughed into the silence, full-toothed, and a number of the pimps joined in, nervously. He waited for the laughter to subside, then began.

'In a different set of circumstances, what I am about to propose to you all might be called "trade union", "industry body", or something like that. Now wouldn't that be easy?' He was holding the broken glass stem aloft, and seemed for a moment fascinated by it. Then he returned his attention to the men. 'You all know why we're here. We're here because our livelihoods are under threat by the app they call Pimple. Every day we see more girls sign up, turning their backs on us, and every girl that does is another pound from our pockets. Many are setting up on their own, using the app, and some are leaving the game altogether. They're not running from one of us, gentlemen, they're running from all of us. This cannot continue. We must make a stand.'

There was a general ripple of approval, although there was also reluctance to concede seniority by making too great a show of enthusiasm.

'The upstarts who run the app have hidden themselves away. Try as we might – and believe me we've tried – we haven't been able to track them down.' He paused, aware of the limited powers of comprehension among many of the invitees. 'It pains me to say it… but violence is our only hope. We must show the world why it needs us. The more that women are attacked for using the Pimple app, the more the pressure will mount.' There was a wild glint in Smith's eyes. He gesticulated brashly, still holding the glass stem, now like the hilt of a rapier. His audience sat spellbound.

'You've all seen the way these people write.' Here he was referring to the creators of Pimple. 'They're a bunch of fucking idealists, without the slightest idea about how our world works. What do they know? Let me tell you – put them under pressure, they'll crack. Bruise up a few bitches and they'll crack.' Smith stopped for a moment to straighten himself out. 'We have to be together in this. And make no mistake, we are fighting for our lives.'

Smith sat down, and the spell was broken. Several men spoke loudly at the same time. Then a half-dozen voices overlapped, then more. A few men left the room. Those that stayed soon settled. Between them they talked more evenly about the practicalities of a plan. Resolutions were made. They would be known as the Fist. They would work together to unhinge the Pimple network, bludgeoning their way back to prominence. Things would return to the way they were. They would reverse the flow of change.

15

Gold Rush

Sasha's vanity was a constant point of frustration for Elena. Her friend would spend hours fussing over her hair, or the painting of her eyelids. She had a handheld flip mirror that was always open. Elena had come to hate it.

'Would you put that thing away?' she snapped one day.

'No can do, honey. Got a guy coming up,' said Sasha.

'Always have.'

It was true that Sasha always seemed to have a guy coming up. Elena's were less regular, but paid better. It worked out that the two women earned about the same money, and they were both earning a lot.

An endless line of men shuffled inconspicuously in and out of the tiny flat. The atmosphere had darkened. The men had started to mix socially, having made too many hallway passes to avoid each other. What had begun with awkward nods had transitioned into conversation. Soon they were chatting freely in the flat's claustrophobic lounge.

The sex happened in the bedroom. Elena had her bed in the corner and Sasha had a mattress on the floor. The gap between the two was around the size of two female feet. Sasha's punters had been the first to coalesce, probably because there were more of them. Elena's better-off customers were initially too cautious to converse, and rarely had cause to hang around anyway.

For weeks now, Elena had been almost entirely selective about when she worked, and who she worked with. She was making more than enough money to get by, and although she could see the appeal of ramping things up, she couldn't quite face doing it.

But the poisonous atmosphere in the flat was beginning to take its toll on her. Soon enough her men were chatting to each other and then to Sasha's customers. Next they were asking for drinks while they waited, and then for permission to smoke. Then they stopped asking. The little flat – the symbol of her liberty – was gradually deteriorating into something like a brothel. And Elena was becoming swept up in it.

'Get out!' she cried one day, when she arrived home to find Sasha on the sofa, plastic champagne flute in hand, laughing with a pair of faceless men. 'Get out, now, go on! Get out!'

Barely a week and a half later, she found herself on that same sofa, clutching a similar vessel, surrounded by the same sort of men. Where once they allowed their guests a drink, they began to allow drugs. It was a seamless progression that Elena couldn't remember agreeing to, but suddenly it was entirely ordinary and would have been almost ridiculous to object to. She began to join in, even to enjoy herself. She worked more regularly; after all, she was more numbed to the work.

One evening she was slumped into the grubby sofa beside a man. His shirt was unbuttoned, exposing a hairy belly. Music was playing and cigar smoke filled the room. Sasha and two other men were dancing.

'Come dance, Elena.'

'I don't want to dance.' Her words were weak. 'I don't want to dance.'

'Come dance.'

'No.'

'Don't be shy, baby!' shouted one of the two men. 'Join us!'

'No. I want the air.'

Things seemed to be running away from her. The room was slowly overturning itself, without ever quite managing to tip upside down. The hairy man alongside her was doubled over, snorting a line of cocaine from the tabletop.

Her mind was moving from body to body. There seemed to be an endless trail of bodies. Bodies above her, bodies beneath her. She felt as though she was suffocating. There was no air left to drink; it was all just smoke and flesh. She was vaguely aware of yet another body next to her own, and of an arm draped across her shoulders, and of a nearby drink. The smell of chemicals filled her nostrils and climbed.

She shivered into consciousness, stood up and felt her way towards the door, past the protesting bodies. She stumbled along the corridor to the fire escape. She pounded hazily up four flights of stairs and to the entrance to the roof.

Then she was outside in the bright night. She leaned against a wall that was thick with graffiti. The stars overhead were bright, and yet somehow there was a light rain falling. Elena pressed her palm against her forehead and felt the water flattening.

She felt as though she had been stuck in the flat for many years, and had forgotten the rain and the wind. She nudged a little way along the wall. There was a fuzzy sensation in her mouth and a lightness to her stomach. Her eyes were painfully tired.

The rainfall intensified. Her slim frame convulsed. She doubled over at the waist, vomiting with a violence that threatened to split her oesophagus. She was on all fours. It felt as though she would retch herself to death.

She knew, even then, in such a state as she was in, that if she did not die she would change the way she lived.

16

The Wild Horse

The two women sat outside Packs – an airy, angular café in central London. Inside, an impressive array of cakes and pastries were displayed on a wooden canvas by the counter. The surfaces were mostly bare, save for a hefty steaming coffee machine and a busy till. The furniture looked as though it had been made in a carpentry class for beginners, as did the rickety cutlery holders, but such was the fashion. Each of them had a flimsy clipboard to hand, each one with a greasy menu clipped. Annie was wearing big, round sunglasses in the cool sunshine.

'I watched a documentary on the Beeb last night. The one about the brothel. Have you seen it?' asked Veronica

'No. I haven't seen that one,' replied Annie.

'I found it deeply troubling.'

'I can imagine.'

'It was about an entirely legal brothel in Nevada, near Reno...' explained Veronica.

'I shot a man in Reno...' sang Annie.

'... called the Wild Horse.'

'... Just to watch him die. When I hear that whistle blowin'...'

'Anyway,' continued Veronica. 'It's run by a multi-millionaire property developer and his wife – who used to be a prostitute herself. The first ten minutes of the programme depicted a better way of doing things, and I kind of bought into it. The women working there had pretty decent rooms, and were well fed. The amenities weren't bad. It even had a gym on site. They seemed pretty upbeat about things too. They endorsed the idea that the Wild Horse was a nicer style of brothel. They were making a lot of money and for the most part they seemed fairly happy.'

'Sounds interesting,' said Annie.

'Ten minutes in, it's all changed. For the first time you actually witness the point of purchase. Women no older than twenty are paraded in their knickers for men never younger than forty to pick and choose from. Most of the men are actually older than that. They pick a winner, and there are a few pleasantries to observe, maybe a drink, and then they get right down to it. Some of the women have fifteen different men in a single night.'

'Horrendous.'

'And you see how they are afterwards,' said Veronica. She seemed barely to be addressing the words to Annie. 'They don't seem so keen for the cameras anymore. They aren't nearly as enthusiastic about the place or about their trade, and I felt like a fool for overlooking the ugliness of the whole thing.' She sipped at her drink, glancing over the rim of the cup at Annie, who was gazing absently in the other direction.

Annie felt a pang of déjà vu, only it was not quite déjà vu; it was whatever the inversion of that sensation is.

Veronica pressed on. 'The owners were the worst part – the developer and his wife. They seemed utterly convinced, as if they'd brainwashed themselves, that they were doing a damn good thing, that the Wild Horse was an Eden for working girls. And they acted as if they were all one big happy family. Yet they spied on the girls through peep holes in the walls when they were negotiating with the punters to stop them pocketing any extra.'

Annie's gaze was still fixed on something far away.

'Are you even listening?' asked Veronica.

'I am,' said Annie.

'Any of this sound familiar?'

'Not remotely.'

'Annie, you know that I've been worried about various aspects of the app. But lately I've been getting more and more uncomfortable about what the app is – with what it's fundamentally designed to do. Don't you ever feel that?'

Annie now turned to face her friend. 'Never,' she said, flatly. 'You already know what I'm going to say. I came to terms with what the app is when we started this. I wouldn't have set about it in the first place if I hadn't, and I won't start to doubt myself now. Not when we've come so far.'

'I don't know that I want to go any further,' said Veronica, breaking eye contact with her friend.

Annie flailed a dismissive palm and rose to her feet. 'I'm going to order. Have you decided?'

Veronica shook her head.

The road alongside the café was completely clear, with traffic running fluidly in both directions. But parked up in rows on either side of the street were Prius upon Prius upon Prius – an armada of Uber cars. They had positioned themselves in this way in direct mockery of a recent demonstration by their aged counterparts – London's black cab drivers – who had arranged themselves in the same sort of formation, only planted slap-bang in the middle of the road. By clogging up the city's arteries, their intention had been to protest against their livelihoods being impinged on by Uber. In the event, passers-by were less than sympathetic; those caught in the queues, less so still.

Several months later, under mounting pressure from dusty old trade bodies, Transport for London dreamed up a range of measures to stymie the free rein of Uber drivers in the city. An online petition protesting against these measures attracted hundreds of thousands of signatures from customers overnight. But the pièce de résistance was the mock protest that was now in full flow in the streets outside the café.

When black cab drivers feel threatened, they block up the streets in fear. Uber drivers, on the other hand, stage their protest from the pavements. It was clear to see whose backs were against the wall. It was rare for Annie and Veronica to be lured away from Café Craft in Fulham, but this event had managed it.

That night, Annie had a dream in which the users of her own app rose up in protest – although on waking, she couldn't quite remember why. All she recalled was the glory of woman after woman arising from the digital plane, joining hands in union, in the flesh, fighting for their right to exist.

17

Tim Nestler

According to his social media accounts, Tim Nestler was a 'tech evangelist'. Quite what he meant by that, Warren was unsure. Nestler had long since gained entry into the 500+ connections club on the business-orientated social network LinkedIn. He had an absolutely dizzying number of skills listed on his LinkedIn profile, many of which had been heavily endorsed. These so-called skills were largely intangible things like 'Entrepreneurship' or 'Innovation'. Above all, he appeared to pride himself on a perceived flair for oratory.

Now Nestler was sitting uncomfortably in the lounge area of a bustling police station in Holborn. He was wearing a furry sort of blazer over a dark blue shirt. His trousers were exceptionally tight. He wore Italian leather boots. The thin frame of his spectacles was patterned like leopard skin.

'Mr Nestler.' Warren approached the confused-looking man with a hand outstretched. David and Grace were in tow. 'Thank you so much for coming in to see us.'

'Sure. What's this all about?' he asked.

'Hoping you might be able to help us. Can I get you anything to drink? Tea? Coffee?' asked Warren.

'Tea, please. Green tea if you have it,' said Tim.

'David, would you mind?'

'Pleasure.'

David shuffled off reluctantly. Warren and Grace sat down at either side of their guest – the three points of a squashed isosceles.

'I'll cut straight to the chase, Mr Nestler. We understand that a suspect of ours has been using – DCX, is it? – to buy digital currency.

They're buying the stuff using dirty money, and we're unable to track that money once it's been exchanged.'

'I see,' said Tim. He had a soft German accent.

'I'd like you to bar our suspect from using the platform,' said Warren.

Nestler looked down his large, pointed nose at Warren. He seemed to consider the request an affront to his honour. He was a tech evangelist, after all, and a world-renowned one at that.

Eventually he spoke. 'And how would that help you?'

'It will force them into contacting your team for assistance,' said Grace, jumping into the fray. 'And we'll be waiting to trace the call when they do.'

Nestler jolted as though he had been blindsided by a blow to the head. 'It's out of the question,' he said.

Warren hadn't been expecting much resistance. There was a lengthy pause. Nestler held his chin up, defiantly high. Warren began to apply pressure to his fastened fists with his thumbs, as if squeezing on spring-coiled clips. He squeezed according to a familiar pattern – once with the right thumb, twice with the left, once more with the right, and switch, once with the left, twice with the right, finish on the left. His temper was pulsating to the rhythm of his fists. Nestler had pushed, and Warren was aware of himself shaping to push back. But before he could, Grace intervened once more.

'Are you aware of your legal responsibilities, as the operator of a currency exchange?' she asked.

'I am fully aware,' said Tim scornfully.

'I'm not so sure you are. The situation that we've just described to you constitutes a form of money laundering. There are no two ways about it. You have a responsibility, as the proprietor of DCX, to make every effort to prevent such activity. We have just brought such a matter to your attention. My strong suggestion' – Grace paused for dramatic effect, having got a little carried away – 'is that you respond accordingly.'

Nestler wilted in wonderfully haughty style. He fixed Grace with a stare that he must have imagined to be intimidating. His spindly legs, which had been folded one atop the other, were now set neatly side by side. Before answering, he withdrew a pristine handkerchief from his inside breast pocket and blew his nose, in a way that was so considered that he might have been playing an instrument.

'I suppose you have a point there, detective.'

The rapidity of the about-turn was laughable. His principles had been laid to waste in less than a minute. Nestler was only ever, after all, what one might describe as circumstantially principled. He was well practised in justifying his pivots.

'Now that you put it that way, I see what you mean. I would of course be delighted to assist you in your investigation.'

'Excellent!' exclaimed Warren, clapping his hands and standing.

'How do we proceed?' asked Nestler.

'We'll tell you what we know about the user,' said Grace. 'Should be pretty easy to spot. Once you've blocked them from transacting, you should expect some sort of communication from a shell email account. Ignore this.'

Nestler nodded.

'You'll need to hang on the phones. Eventually they'll call you, I'm sure of it. When they do, we'll be on hand to trace the call.'

'Sounds simple enough,' said Nestler.

The trap was set.

18

In the Media

As with the majority of disruptive technologies, Pimple was subject to three distinct phases of media scrutiny.

First comes the honeymoon period, when the idea and its effect enter the minds of a handful of enthusiastic and ambitious journalists, who become ambassadorial in their interest. The idea impregnates these generally youthful spirits and soon develops its hosts into specialists in an emergent field of journalism. Their careers are for a time buoyed by the attachment. The quality of their coverage – they being wary of the connection – inevitably deteriorates. They become less scrupulous, more easily blinded by company spin.

It is then that the hardened journalists, who have kept their hands clean, descend. The specialists are swept aside, accused of having consumed the Kool-Aid. Painfully considered probings of the technology's processes and infrastructure begin to crop up in the serious reader segments. Everything is suddenly coloured by a deep and indomitable cynicism. The readers of the print versions of special features sections nod knowingly as they devour the latest exposé on a company that had attempted to impinge upon bank monopoly, or to upset the publishing industry.

The third phase comprises a tailing off of interest, in one of two ways. The technology in question weathers the storm of phase two, and as such is no longer seen to be innovative; in which case it becomes considerably less interesting to journalists and readers alike. Alternatively, the spotlight proves altogether too bright, and the company buckles under a succession of public outings, ultimately collapsing. In the latter case, the company name appears subsequently only as an example of why budding entrepreneurs *ought to know better*.

For Pimple, being what it was, both the fervour of phase one and the scepticism of phase two were greatly accentuated.

The enduring appeal of the seemingly outdated in, say, fashion, made sense to Annie. She could just about bring herself to admit that there were certain sectors where the old ways might, in fact, be best. The paperback had long since been rendered practically inferior by the Kindle and other technologies like it. And yet the paperback heart beat on, resolute and regular, undimmed. Sentimentality had saved it.

Annie used to lie awake at night, fretting over the idea that this same style of sentimental impairment might forever preserve the banking industry. For all the anti-bank feeling that had been stored up in the wake of the global financial crisis, there was a familiarity to those high street structures that Annie feared would forever keep them intact.

The morning headlines now invoked in her a measure of that same fear, only this time it was attached – bizarrely – to facilitators of the sex trade.

Violence towards users of the Pimple app was spiking. The network could weed out wrongdoing, but only if it had enough time enough to do so. New users on the buyer side – if prone to misdeeds – soon developed a score that identified them as undesirable. Annie and Veronica didn't need to ban such men because the app self-moderated. Women saw a low score and recoiled.

But there was one major flaw, and that was that the network could only learn through pain, and that pain had to be felt by somebody. There was simply no way around it. It was the facet of the app that made Veronica most uncomfortable, as she repeatedly told Annie. Annie tried to manage her friend's misgivings by advising her that they were paying a short-term price for tremendous long-term gain, and that the network was simply experiencing 'growing pains'. But that line of argument was faltering.

The growing pains were becoming increasingly difficult to stomach. What had initially amounted to the occasional incident of roughness or effective theft had in recent weeks transformed into serious physical abuse. Those women who were unfortunate enough to sit at the lower end of Pimple's quality spectrum were inevitably the ones who bore the brunt of this. They were taking chances on unrated, first-time users, and more and more they were paying a heavy price for the risk. Photographs of black-eyed, bludgeoned sex workers were popping up in steadily more prominent positions within the press.

'We've got to make that help button more obvious...' mumbled Annie one day.

'Yes,' said Veronica, who was sitting with her head in her hands in their headquarters looking decidedly weary. 'I can't make sense of the data. It's natural to assume that new users would be responsible for the bulk of whatever violence occurs, but the sheer volume of violent individuals that are suddenly signing up is inexplicable.'

'Any unifying features between them?' asked Annie. She was coiled up on a pouffe, toying with redesigns of the Pimple logo.

'Only that most offenders are in the one-and-done category,' said Veronica. 'Nobody will accept their custom after the red flags have been raised.'

Annie looked up from her tablet and cocked her head. There was a pause while she thought. Then her eyes widened. 'Sounds like we're up against some sort of co-ordinated action.'

'How do you mean?' asked Peter Froome, who was working sleepily alongside Veronica.

'Think about it!' exclaimed Annie. 'These people are effectively suicide bombing the network. Why? What do they have to gain? If you were minded to make a random attack, the worst possible way to do it would be on a network that registers your personal details and tracks your location. No. These attacks are linked all right. But by what?'

The answer was that the Fist had been piling resources into discrediting and thereby dismantling the network. Thugs in the employ of pimps from all over the city were being offered a fee for each successful battery. Few were able to manage more than one, but there was no shortage of thick-skulled thugs in London; one beating apiece would do. The more pictures of these beatings cropped up in the media, the more public sentiment turned, like a gigantic frigate changing course.

The apex of negativity towards the app came that very day. Annie absorbed the morning headlines in disbelief.

A pimp – who had asked, for obvious reasons, to remain anonymous – had given an interview to a *Wired* journalist, excerpts of which could now be found in most of the major papers. The unnamed pimp had spoken out against the Pimple app, denouncing it as an unregulated scourge and as dangerous for women, while pointing to himself and his associates as the more secure alternative.

Journalists were not blind to his self-interest, of course, nor were they deaf to the offensiveness of his existence, but he was not the current object of their attentions. They were caught up in the wash of anti-Pimple feeling. Most of the articles adopted a kind of *lesser of two evils* slant. Annie read them all, word for word.

'*The old ways work best!*' shouted Annie. '*There's a reason they keep to the shadows. Perhaps it's time this disruptor was disrupted.* Have you ever heard such rubbish?' She yelled and paced around the room, flinging from one paper to the next, while Veronica remained conspicuously quiet.

The honeymoon phase was well and truly over.

19

Brunch and Murder

Never in the long and winding history of London had brunch been quite so fashionable. The weekend mornings saw faster flows of Prosecco than had ever before been witnessed – drawn from what were frequently advertised as 'bottomless' reserves. The poached egg had reached the zenith of its trendiness, as had the once wholly humble 'smashed' avocado and the sourdough slice.

It was among the educated youth that this interlude between breakfast and lunch had found its niche. South and central London were its crucibles; the up and coming borough of Balham was perhaps its headquarters. Like prospectors in a gold rush, eatery after eatery had sprung up in the hope of diverting the raging river of yuppies. The uniformity was staggering. It was truly a wonder that any one venue rose to prominence at the expense of another, and yet one had.

Uncle Butler proved to be the favourite of the hungry Balham masses. Every weekend the queue wound out of the entrance and off around the corner. Its competitors leeched off the inevitable spillover, becoming quite successful in their own right.

But on one especially bright morning in May, there were no queues whatsoever. Instead there were crowds, there was the flashing of photography and there was a limply drawn police cordon.

In one of the bought-to-let flats that sat a floor up from Uncle Butler there lived a girl named Maisie. Maisie was a Scot who had come to London to study. That was all that could be discerned about her from her online profile.

Whenever a new vendor signed up to the Pimple app, they received a notice of warning, advising them that first-time users of the platform were at greater risk than others of running afoul of hazardous customers. The headline warning was printed in big, bold lettering. There were also several paragraphs of explanatory text, and a box that had to be ticked. This feature put some girls off altogether, but the majority were undeterred, in much the same way that a smoker seldom declines a cigarette because of a gruesome picture on the packet.

On her own Pimple debut, which had taken place the previous evening, Maisie had proceeded with barely a cursory glance through the warning text. Statistically, her hastiness should not have cost her.

Emerson Smith had waited at the entrance to the flats. It was dark enough that even his closest associates would have struggled to identify him. The doorway was wedged between Uncle Butler and a Threshers store.

The door creaked open. White moonlight laid itself upon his back, brightening his periphery, but enshrouding his face. He kept almost impossibly still. The outline of his face was blurred by a thick beard. Maisie led him inside by the hand; Emerson followed. They picked their way up the stairs, into the girl's flat and on into the bedroom.

'How do you want to do this?' she asked.

Emerson declined to respond, but studied her intensely. Maisie looked awkward; he relished her discomfort. The act that had so seamlessly been agreed to via the app now seemed difficult for either party to initiate, or even to imagine. It was his debut too, after all. Now that he was here, teetering on the verge of it, everything felt strange, almost dream-like, but he was content to ride along with the sensation.

'Well?' said Maisie, in a voice that worked to sound assertive, but failed.

He advanced on her. Maisie, apparently imagining that their engagement was about to begin, went limp. The lights were out in the room; what natural light there was caught her white teeth and the dead whites of her eyes.

Adrenaline coursed in his veins. The girl looked suddenly frightened and at the same time his long fingers wound their way around her neck, but in fact the two things happened quite independently of one another. She mouthed wordless sounds. Her bare hamstrings were pressed up against the bed and she tried to lean backwards, seemingly imagining that they would both give way and collapse onto it in a passionate embrace.

But still his hands were wound around her neck, and now they were beginning to constrict, closing off her airway. Fear turned into panic before his eyes. She took a hold of his arms and tried to dislodge them, but soon found that she couldn't.

'Heretic,' hissed Emerson, in a long, seething whisper.

'Stop,' she mouthed, but no sound came. She couldn't speak.

It was by now clear that she knew what was happening. She struck at him with her fists and with her knees but the blows landed as if muffled by thick layers of cloth. She looked to have been overcome by a strange sensation. Emerson made a mental slideshow of her transition. Her wilting face.

It was deeply unfair, he thought, how much stronger he was than her. After all, there was no reason that he should be. It was a critical and decisive biological advantage and it seemed so desperately unfair. He pored over her, considering it. Her blows began to soften. Life was leaving her, or she was leaving life – he couldn't tell which.

Her body became entirely relaxed. Then she was gone, and Emerson stood alone in the darkness.

20

Bicyclists and Breakups

The bicycle lane was bustling. The pedals whirred like crickets. The bicyclists themselves were especially feisty. They were vascular, wiry, with hooked noses, strapped to bottles and backpacks, squeezed into garish, spandex costumes – an endless amateur-hour peloton.

The heat of the day, and the leisurely walkers that came with it, were a clear source of disturbance. Time and again feet were falling into the bicycle lane, in flagrant breach of the spacing assigned to each group. The bicyclists barked pugnaciously at the invaders as they whooshed by, swerving dramatically an inch or two to one side.

Annie in particular was drawing the ire of the cyclists as she ran along the bike lane towards the box-shaped building with the colourful, bulging balconies. She had woken that morning to the news of Maisie McCaffery's murder.

Veronica would be beside herself. She needed to be by her side. It was now nearing ten, and the sun was reared up mightily over the bustling road. Annie looked a mess. She was wearing a heavily creased, loose-fitting dress and a pair of sandals, and her hair was more unkempt than ever. She was sweating.

She burst into Flat 712 and found Veronica waiting with her back to the door. She was wearing a hoodie and had the hood up; giving her the look of a tombstone. She stood up as Annie entered. She had clearly been crying. There was no makeup to smudge, but her brown eyes were bloodshot and her normally pristine face looked wearied, as if she had aged a great deal over the past six months without Annie noticing. Annie ran to her, and Veronica allowed herself to be hugged.

'Oh Ron,' she said. 'Veronica, I'm so sorry. I'm so, so sorry.'

'It's over, Annie.'

Annie continued to hug her friend.

'Annie, it's over.' Veronica pushed her away gently.

'What do you mean?' asked Annie.

'This is it. This goes no further.'

Annie stepped back from Veronica and composed herself. 'I... I don't understand.'

'I can't be a part of this anymore,' said Veronica. 'I want nothing more to do with the app. I'm going home now and I'm not coming back here. I've spoken with Peter. He feels the same way. You can keep using the space if you want to. We're out.'

Veronica spoke very calmly. Her words sounded carefully rehearsed, and she delivered them with frightening intensity.

Annie was plotting a response, wary of her friend's fragility. She knew what was at stake. 'Veronica...'

'You can't talk me out of this one. I'm decided. I'm leaving right now.' Veronica marched past Annie towards the door.

Annie scuttled to intercept her, pulling at her arm. 'You can't leave.' She was almost hysterical, her blue eyes popping. 'We're so close. I can't do this without you, you know that. Veronica, we're so close.'

'What does that even mean?' yelled Veronica, swirling to face her friend. 'Close? Close to what?'

'We just need more time, Ron. The network needs more time.'

'To what?'

'To mature,' answered Annie, and then, triumphantly: 'To blossom!'

'This is what you do, Annie!' exclaimed Veronica. 'You cover over the cracks with big words and grand visions of the future, and you either don't know or you don't care what's happening all around you!'

'Ron, these growing pains...'

'A woman *died*, Annie!' roared Veronica.

Annie recoiled. She had never seen her so ferociously angry.

A tear had rolled clear of Veronica's eyelid. 'Growing pains,' she repeated, as if in disbelief, then took her chance and headed though the door, slamming it behind her.

Annie was reeling. She went over to the table and slumped with her head in her hands. She drove her fingers into her thicket of brown hair and wound and twisted them through it. She could feel that old familiar yearning come creeping up her spine. Her taste buds began to tingle as if after a deep and lengthy slumber. She could think of nothing but drink.

She began to pace about the room, flinging thoughts like speculative anchors in all directions, desperate for something to catch. Her thirst was pervasive, colouring everything. There was no escape. She felt herself drifting towards to the door and became scared. She was close to conceding defeat.

Then her eyes fell upon a note on the table and she wondered how she had missed it. She lunged for it. It was from Veronica, eloquently explaining her reasons for leaving Pimple. Annie cried silently as she read.

The note advised Annie to abandon the app. Should she choose to press on, however, there was a 90-page operating manual on the table – which Veronica had prepared in anticipation of her departure. The manual included a plan for winding down the platform responsibly. Annie flicked through it numbly. There were parts of it that she could scarcely make sense of.

In the wider world of technology, an advisory firm named Gartner had come up with a graphic representation of the typical firm's 'hype cycle'. The graph was an attempt to distil the trajectories of some of the world's hottest technology stocks – including the likes of Facebook, Twitter and Apple – into a single, snaking line. The graph's two axes were labelled 'visibility' and 'maturity'. The line of trajectory ran by the following pit stops: 'technology trigger', 'peak of inflated expectations', 'trough of disillusionment', 'slope of enlightenment' and finally up to the hallowed 'plateau of productivity'. Pimple was now firmly rooted in the third of these generic stop-offs. Annie was determined to climb.

21

Taking a Stand

'Too far.' Viola slammed a palm against her thigh for emphasis. The women around her were in a frenzy. Elena was among them, as was Sasha, although the two had separated. 'Too damn far.'

Their meeting was taking place in a cavernous conference room. There were now so many women in attendance at the meet-ups that suitable venues were hard to find. There were perhaps as many as 400 women stuffed into the space. Not too many places in London could hold such numbers, but Pimple had made emergency arrangements.

They were in an old brewery on Draper Street. Usually, the place was dressed up for awards dinners, or for conferences where companies paid for 2×2 metre areas within which to erect a table and promotional banners ('taking a stand', in corporate parlance).

Today the place had been left bare, save for a few chairs and some roaming microphones, which the women passed around.

Viola clutched one now. 'The girl who was killed was twenty-two years old.' Several women in Viola's entourage were brandishing newspapers in the air behind her. Maisie's death was front-page news. 'Just twenty-two. The time has come to put a stop to this. Strength can only be met with strength.'

Viola was a naturally large and athletic-looking woman. Her movements were prowling and sure. 'Pimple was a start for us. It gave us a taste of freedom. But now the pimps are trying to snatch that freedom from us. Who here has heard of the Fist?'

She gestured around with her free hand. There was a roar from the audience. An overly enthusiastic thug had given away the group's existence a few weeks before.

'For those of you who have not, they're a group of pimps who banded together with a single goal in mind: to tear down Pimple, to claw us back! Their plan was and remains simple: to intimidate, to attack and now it would seem to kill any woman who dares to use the app. It's terrorism. We are being terrorised!'

Each word left a ringing in the ears. The room was at fever pitch. Women were jumping around in rage.

'Will we be scared into submission?'

The crowd swelled up in denial.

'Will we abandon the app? Hell no, we will not. But we cannot continue to put our lives on the line. And so, I urge you, use the app. I implore you to use it. But arm yourself however you can – guns, knives, whatever you can find. Let us never allow what happened to Maisie to happen again.'

Viola tossed her microphone to a nearby supporter. Much applause and feet banging ensued, lasting for well over a minute.

Elena could feel a pocket of support amassing behind her. She had feared that this might happen. She glanced around to see familiar faces: Caroline and the angry-faced woman from the wall at their first meeting – her support, in particular, had come as a surprise. The women nodded or stared their encouragement. Somebody thrust a microphone into her hand. She was moved into the middle of the group – or perhaps the crowd rearranged itself around her. She had given some thought to this; in fact, there was a very small part of her that longed for it. She stole all the seconds she could before raising the microphone to her lips.

'I'm sorry,' she began. Her eyes had not fallen on any one person in particular. 'I'm sorry, Viola, but I cannot agree.'

Viola's supporters again turned wild, arms and voices raised. But Viola herself watched thoughtfully.

'Pimple is under fire in the press,' continued Elena. 'We see it every day. If we take to the streets with knives in our jeans, we'll turn the app into a war zone. Public opinion will only get worse.' She paused. 'The better course now is to show our support for the app, to make our voices heard far and wide. We need to educate the public about what's really going on. We need to tell them about the Fist, talk to them about our experiences with the app, and about why the pimps are reacting this way. We need to show that the pimps are the broken ones – not us, and not Pimple.'

Elena felt conflicted. She had made numerous resolutions to cut all ties to Pimple and to begin a new life. She hadn't managed it yet, but she felt certain that she would soon. And yet here she was, preaching a more moderate style of support for the network. The hypocrisy was not lost on her, but even so she felt compelled to counter Viola's radicalism. Pimple was about the 'democratisation of prostitution' – its mysterious founders had reeled off the phrase a thousand times. Now the representatives in that democracy were beginning to emerge.

'I have nothing more to say,' said Elena, handing the microphone to the nearby Sasha and stepping out of the circle. There was moderate applause, mixed in with much murmuring.

'You're right.' The woman whose face was a constant scowl had followed her out of the circle. 'You're right about the app. You got my vote, girl. I got your back. I'm Sadie, by the way.'

She extended a hand and Elena shook it, unsure exactly what was going on, but nonetheless uneasy. It seemed it was exactly her reticence to hold authority that made some so keen that she should have it.

'Thank you,' she said, sinking further into the crowd.

22

The Mural

It was one of those parts of town that has gone to rot; where every third shop sign is bereft of its full complement of lettering. Stray skips were overflowing with debris. Ahead were the remnants of a bustling market, its residual juices still trickling into the gutters. Tramps and beggars cropped up with saddening regularity, barely bothering to raise their creaking bones in plea to passers-by. A man crouched in a cardboard box, reading feverishly from the Quran.

And yet, here were row upon row of freshly planted 'Sold' signs and a gaggle of girls in high-waisted skirts, skin on show, marked out by plaits and pretty piercings. Bars and eateries – alive with the bustle of youth – had muscled in between the corner shop and bookies, and up ahead beneath the slowly sagging bridge. Inane trifles were spluttered over between groups of woollen-collared men with audaciously coiffed hair, open shirts and conspicuously tatty trainers. The southeastern scoff hung thick as smog.

Such was the flagrancy of the cultural incursion that Annie was later compelled to put pen to page. The result was entitled 'The Ballad of Brixton':

> Shimmy through the fleshy throng,
> Past the drunken busker's song.
> Past the piled rubbish sacks, grip the nostrils tight.
> Clear the bridge's dusty rumble, take the second right.
>
> Down the burned-out alley,
> The stalls are shutting soon.
> Skip between the scattered veg,
> Elude the touter's croon.

Past the little fishmonger's,
The thousand milky eyes.
Brush between the scarves and shawls,
Press a palm to either thigh.

Veer into the shop-row crack,
Dimly lit and scribbled thick.
Tiptoe round the fallen path
Where pipework laces into brick.

Across the road to Fancies,
A trendy, bare-brick haunt.
Trade in chatter, high of mind,
What woes we know, we leave behind;
Onward to a blurred and jolly jaunt!

Cavort the cavernous, strobe-lit shell,
Contort to trumpet, trombone, drum.
To where or what we are, to hell!
To beat, to body, we succumb.

Totter to the taxi rank,
By the beggars, by the tramps.
Worry not for jingling pots, for croaking pleas, or card-
board cots.
Think not of the biting chill, the showing bones, the grim
have-nots.
Loiter by the sold sign,
The second one along.
A fuzzy baseline ringing,
Now unattached to song.

Our gaze now fades to darkness,
The evening's slide complete.
The scouring of a sparkling sink,
A fair-weather defeat.

Annie passed the frontmost houses of a deep and warren-like estate.

Mere strides later, she entered a street lined with Victorian town-houses, then passed a chained-up granite garage advertising bargain prices. She walked beneath the shade of a large fern, which was teeming with chattering, lime-green parrots. There were colossal, hive-like tower blocks looming through the distant mist. Only a hundred or so years before they would have stood as monuments to the ingenuity of man. Now hundreds of miscellaneous objects clung to their sides. Towels, flags and satellite dishes: humanity flat-packed into the sky.

Annie's mind was never far from Maisie McCaffery, the girl who had been murdered while using Pimple. For several weeks she had slept terribly, haunted by visions of the girl's face, which continued to surface in the papers. But Annie had somehow managed to bend her grief into motivation. She felt now, more than ever, that she owed it to Maisie and others like her to make good on Pimple's promise to the world: to deliver a better kind of prostitution.

She was now nearing her quarry. She turned left off the high street and down a quiet side road, which forked into two, and then into two again. Taking the left each time, she soon noticed a slight slowing of the pavement traffic up ahead, a kind of clot upon the walkway.

The subject of people's distraction appeared to have been fixed to the base of a canvas-like granite slab that belonged to a roadside house. So seamless was the great grey face that it looked to have been forged from the clean shearing away of one half of the building. Plastered upon the slate, sure enough, was the graphic that Annie had been looking for.

In jet-black print graffiti was a simply sketched but clearly discernible man and woman – both blindfolded. Between them was a grotesquely caricatured pimp, in colour, wearing a fur-lined coat that had frothed up around his bulging face.

That was the first sight yielded by the gradually passing bodies. Next, to the left, came a solitary greater-than symbol. Finally, a second human duo, this time in colour – one a fruity-looking woman, the other a bashful-looking man. Here the middle ground was held by a block black mobile phone, its use clearly demonstrated by a crescendo of curves that spouted from its upper-right corner.

Annie stood back from the thing, beaming, absorbing its full effect. She took a photograph. The work had first surfaced on the Pimple forums, later finding its way even as far as the national press as the accompanying image in a feature article on the app and a selection of its patrons.

'The problem with it is,' said a stout, vole-like man in a tightly drawn duffle coat, tutting as he wheeled his wife away, 'that it glorifies the whole business.' Then, with the precision of a Roman orator, he added: 'Prostitution is now and will always be immoral and wrong.'

Annie's bones strained against her skin, willing her to interject.

But the presumed wife, equally short and stout, plucked up instead. 'But perhaps less so, Howard – with power in the women's hands.'

Annie could have leaped upon her in embrace. 'Attagirl,' she breathed.

The husband offered only a grunt in reply. Soon the pair had pottered laboriously from view. Annie watched them for as long as she could – her mind a lacework of idea and opportunity, a tapestry in flux.

23

A Name to Hang a Case Around

'Have you heard?'

'No.'

'Nothing?'

'Not a thing.'

'Shout for me as soon as you do.'

'Course. Where are you going?'

'Gotta sort something.'

Warren wheeled away from Grace and into the yellow-tinted stairwell. He crashed down two floors and into the bathroom and went straight over to the sink, where he turned on an old-fashioned tap. He was determined that this would be the final furlong in a grossly elongated endeavour.

He slid his long-fingered hands into and out of the stream of icy water. He pressed on the soap dispenser and made a lather of the pink goo. He recommitted both hands to the water and scrubbed one furiously against the other, with real aggression. He paid particularly close attention to his knuckle tops, for it had occurred to him while prowling around upstairs that he may have neglected these on a previous visit. Warren stood there scrubbing for the better part of a minute, like a malfunctioning machine.

The cleansing complete, he carefully removed his purified palms from the running water. He leaned over the sink and turned the tap off with the point of his elbow, which was shielded by two layers of clothing. He used the same elbow to activate the rasping hand dryer. He held his hands in position until they were wholly dry. Then he made his exit, careful all the while never to touch anything with his bare hands.

Once back in the bustle of the station floor, he felt more rational. He was soon touching things again; he convinced himself that this wasn't a problem, now that he had passed through the mythic barrier that was the stairwell door. But all day, bothersome occurrences had been sending him spiralling downwards once more. After fifteen minutes he had nearly lost interest in the sanitation of his hands, and then it struck again.

This time, on his way to seek another update from Grace, he plucked a pen from his colleague Bernie's pen pot because the biros in his own office had been exhausted. Bernie had an excess of pens, but was off sick and thus unable to police the supply. No sooner had Warren done so than the memory of Bernie's sickness stirred. There was every chance of contagion; the pen was probably draped in the invisible green of malady.

Forget it, Warren tried to tell himself. *For God's sake just forget it.* But he could not. Once more he was forced into the stairwell and down unto the purity of the running tap. It was perhaps his tenth visit of the day. He hungered for news, for anything to distract him; in the back of his mind was the belief that it could come only to one with uncontaminated hands. Then there was a rapping at the door.

'Boss! Warren!' Grace burst into the dank-smelling lavatory. Warren had turned the tap off instinctively – with his bare fingers – and was drying his hands in what he considered to be blasé fashion. 'We've got her!'

'Her?' Had he heard Grace correctly? 'Show me!'

The pair bounded up the stairs. Duffin was on the line, sounding extremely flustered. 'Female. Strong Northern Irish accent. Sounded very stressed. We traced the call to a house in Fulham. SW6 1AG.'

'Check the listings,' said Warren, a mad excitement in his eyes.

'Way ahead of you,' she said. There was utter stillness save for the pattering of her fingertips. 'Gotcha. One Miss Annie O'Mahony. She's lived there five years.'

'I want everything you can find on her,' he said, numbly. 'David, get back here as soon as you can.'

'Will do, boss,' panted David.

The line went dead. Warren rubbed his hands together in thoughtful anticipation. 'Find all that you can and get it to me as soon as. I'm going to speak to Payne. We need to move fast on this. She might scare off.'

'Roger,' replied Grace, who was already at one with the computer.

Superintendent Payne had been saying for weeks that Warren was wasting his time and resources on the Pimple case, and that it was merely an exercise in exorcising old demons. She said he needed to refocus his energies on a number of missing persons cases that were all believed to be connected. But this would change all that. Having a name to hang a case around always did.

What Grace turned up in the annals of law and order put their suspicions beyond doubt. Annie O'Mahony was a middle-aged woman from Holywood in County Down, Northern Ireland. She was best known for having founded a company named Millennial Credit – an online marketplace for loans that connected lenders directly to borrowers, thereby cutting out the banks.

Northern Ireland. *Could it really be her? The woman from Soho?* The more he considered it, the more sense it made.

Warren almost burst out laughing at how damned obvious the whole thing now seemed. There was a breadcrumb trail fit to fill a bakery. But in among his excitement and his anxiety over the twirling hands of the clock was another strain of feeling. It was the glow of admiration.

He felt suddenly conflicted. It was only a split-second feeling – a sentimental palpitation – but still, it troubled him. His obsession was wavering at the very moment of its triumph. Now that he knew the identity of this woman – and he was not blind to the fact that her being a woman may have changed matters too – he could not imagine her the way he had hoped to. Until now, when picturing the font of evil that was the Pimple app, Warren had brought to mind the face of Emerson Smith, out of habit. He had almost hoped that it was Smith. That would have made things so much simpler. Now, everything had become muddled into a guerilla-style scrap, with all its battle lines blurred.

24

The Leech

Emerson Smith's existence was fundamentally parasitical, and he had identified at an early stage in the rise of Pimple that he lacked the proper resources for toppling it. He also suspected that Detective Chief Inspector Warren Beckett – a long-time thorn in his side – would be turning his infernal attentions to the app before long. The obvious course, then, was to play the leech again, and acquire a man in Beckett's team.

Through a blend of bribery and coercion, he had followed that course. He referred to his inside man as 'Double D' in all correspondence. Double D was tasked with keeping Smith abreast of any and every development in the ongoing investigation of Pimple – and so he had. Double D had also fanned the flames of his boss's hatred of the app – flames which threatened to waver if left untended.

'Double D.'

The detective spun on the spot. He had been instructed to wait for Smith on a spit of concrete which broke into a creek that ran lazily into the Thames. The water level was low, the water itself stagnant, and algae was climbing the walls that banked the river. Train tracks ran overhead, and the sound of a train was rattling far off in the distance. Tall blocks of modern flats climbed skyward all around, but this concrete spit had been forsaken and was platform only to a derelict warehouse with shattered windows.

Smith's voice floated from the shadows of the warehouse. 'What tidings?'

David Duffin took a step forwards. Benz emerged from the shadows as a large and unexpected shape, like a rock breaking the surface of the sea. He came straight for the detective and patted him down for wires and weaponry. He was clean.

The slighter shape of Smith then emerged, strolling assuredly and languidly towards them. He was wearing an all-black, slim-line suit that looked to be brand new. He laid a hand on each of David's gently trembling shoulders.

'You said it was urgent. What tidings?' Smith repeated.

'Good news.' David spoke through pursed lips, and was panting lightly. 'We've found her. We have a home address.'

Smith's face shifted abruptly from flat to joyful. He let out a loud laugh, and clapped his paid man upon the shoulders.

'Excellent work, D! There's no time to lose. What's the address? Benz! Make a note.'

'It's a house in Fulham. SW6 1AG. You'll need to be quick,' said David.

'Benz, call John. Get Skinny and Tom and the rest of 'em and get to that house.' Benz made as if to dart off, but Smith caught him by the arm and tugged him close, so that their eyes levelled. 'Heaven help you if the feds get there before us.'

He allowed a few seconds for the words to seep in. Then Benz bolted with a litheness unusual for a man of his size.

'Double D.' Smith was smiling and shaking his head in mock disbelief. He placed a single palm on the detective's left shoulder. The absence of the right hand was in itself unnerving. 'What a show you've put on.'

'My niece –'

'Is safe. I give you my word,' said Smith.

David Duffin breathed a deep sigh of relief. Globules of sweat had formed beneath his puffy eyes.

'Thank you,' he said.

Emerson looked him dead in the eyes, a smile still creasing his face. Then, in one smooth and sudden movement, he pulled a broad-bladed knife from somewhere by his side and drove it upward under Duffin's sternum and into his racing heart.

There was a moment of silence as his world wobbled. Then Duffin screamed. Blood was bursting in ribbons from his chest. He was spluttering amid his screams. Lurching heavily backwards, he blindly clutched at the knife handle and drew the blade outwards, and the blood flowed out faster in its absence. He pressed his hands desperately against the wound, trying to stem the flow. It seeped between his fingertips and into the pools that were amassing on the cold ground.

'Help me,' he tried to say, forgetting his audience. 'Call an ambulance.'

Emerson stood motionless, chuckling to himself. 'Double D,' he said again, slowly.

Duffin's suffering continued for less than a minute. He took a knee before the end, and then lay down on his back, perhaps believing that he could better contain the bleeding that way.

Emerson watched until the last breath left his lips, and never moved a muscle, save those required for light laughter. Then he walked over to the slackened body and looked down at it. He collected the knife, covered in blood, and wiped the blade with tissue paper before sheathing and repocketing it. He left the drained corpse of David Duffin where it lay.

The train that had been rattling in the distance sounded nearer now. Benz had cut the wires of all known surveillance cameras in the area. Still, there was every chance that the murder had been witnessed from afar, for the evening was as bright as it was young.

Smith strode away from the scene without a backwards glance. His mind was racing ahead.

25

Collapse

Emerson Smith watched from beyond the tinted windows of a rusted white van. A woman was picking her way up the path towards the marked house in Fulham. She looked concerned, but she wasn't rushing. In the back of the van were four brawny men, who hardly dared to draw breath.

The day was balmy. A light breeze gently ruffled the woman's hair. Smith was sure she was the one. She had the look of an innovator, of a technologist. Soon she arrived at the front gate of the sea-green, semi-detached house. She looked up at it fondly and turned in. Smith brought his men to attention by raising his right hand. Still they were silent.

The house had a tiny garden area out front that was severely overgrown, and yet retained traces of near-comical attempts at ordering. Flecks of an old criss-crossed trellis still peeped through a thicket of ivy. A waist-height statue of a woman wound seamlessly into a birdbath. The water within was murky.

The woman temporarily disappeared down a side passage. Emerson tensed. Then she re-emerged, jangling a set of keys; she tried the lock and the door swung open. She placed a foot assuredly inside, then another.

From nowhere, a calloused hand closed over her mouth and yanked her head backwards. Her neck cricked. Her gaze lurched to find upside down eyes burning through two holes in a balaclava. Instinctively she kicked and thrashed, but she was physically outmatched.

'Get her in!' came the gruff command of Emerson Smith.

The woman began to hyperventilate through her one free nostril. She strained madly and spiritedly. Emerson watched on, convinced now that this was his prize.

'Fucking get her in!' he repeated.

The woman continued to thrash like a hooked and slippery fish. The doors of the large white van were swinging on their rusty hinges. Nobody else was around. The four men managed to bend her halfway into the van. Her glasses fell from her face and crunched under a boot. One of the men was clawing at her ankle; she was kicking at his hands. She shook her lips free of the vice palm that had sealed them and screamed for aid. Then there was a clobbering of knuckle on skull, and the woman fell silent.

Alone at the bar, Annie pored over the papers. It was perhaps the darkest day in the history of the online lending industry. Her old shop, Millennial Credit, had run into serious trouble. Its chief executive, Rory de Sansa, had been embroiled in a mis-selling scandal and fired.

But even that news, sweet though it was, was not so sweet as the first of the morning's victories: namely the resumption of the Pimple machine. The app had temporarily stalled over the weekend because of a glitch in its fee-taking process. Annie had panicked and taken risks, but she had been assured that morning by the staff at DCX that the problem had been ironed out. They said there was nothing to worry about.

Annie was cradling a cocktail – her third – as she pored over the Millennial Credit piece in the day's *Financial Times*. Two victories. Two of the finest. There was something almost unsettling in the upward trajectory of the day. It seemed almost too gaudy, impossible to hold.

A dark, niggling sensation prickled at the deepest recesses of her mind, for some unknown reason. Perhaps it was her enduring estrangement from Veronica. Or perhaps it was that third cocktail. Rarely in the past few years had she chanced three drinks on the bounce; she had imagined they'd make for a nice pairing with the day's news, but a disconnect had grown between them.

Whatever the basis for the feeling, Annie resolved that there would be no fourth glass. And just to cover all bases, she decided to message Veronica, in search of a détente.

As it happened, the old friends remained very much in sync. Veronica replied to say that she was at that very moment heading over to Annie's place, in the hope of catching her. She was turning onto her road now.

Annie's unease lifted. She reminded Veronica of the code to the key safe, and told her to help herself to tea while she waited. She'd be no more than twenty minutes. She wasn't far from home.

26

A Drunken Eureka

Annie was swaying and shaking. Her eyes were glazed. Beyond glazed: they were bloodshot. An excess of liquid was sloshing about in her stomach. It was the cruellest kind of cure for catastrophe, and it was one which, once invoked, required constant upkeep.

For now, the grey veil had been drawn, and she knew nothing. Then, as the mist lifted, she remembered, or half-remembered, her need for oblivion, and reached for another gulp of anaesthetic. But all that is airborne returns to the earth eventually, and Annie was no exception.

She swigged deeply from a bagged vessel. Her head tipped and she lay down flat on the wooden floor of Peter's apartment, the nexus of the Pimple app. Her magnum opus. The bottle fell to the floor by her side and overturned, dripping its contents into the narrow crevice between two planks.

Annie's mind was full of shapes. They were brilliantly coloured and their size was transitory; they loomed large and shrank like poorly tied balloons. Sometimes they broke down altogether and their colours washed into one another. The colours were fluorescent and seemed to simmer in and out of form.

Then a worldly shape intruded: the thin, upright frame of a woman, with straight black hair and clear spectacles. She grew out of the colours as a body from the bog. Annie scrunched her eyelids, moaned quietly and rolled her head to one side. The colours leaped up around the woman and reclaimed her. The rainbow tide reigned once more.

There was a ringing that began quietly. And then a new ringing that scraped against the insides of her skull and hauled her into consciousness. She was in pain. There was physical pain in her head and the deeper, darker pain of her memory, which had starved her out of her sleep, and now besieged her again.

Veronica had been taken. She remembered it now. She remembered the moment of realisation as a great and terrible fall. She recalled the details of the video. They had sent her a video. It had featured her friend and Emerson Smith – about whom she had heard so much at various Pimple meetings that she now longed to forget. He was masked, and his voice sounded distorted, but she was sure it was him. They had been seated alongside one another. He had spoken a great deal. She strained to remember what he had said. Her brain stung with the effort.

She began to recall snippets. Slowly she pieced together the puzzle. *We have Veronica… Wouldn't tell us anything… We know all about you…* She remembered him speaking of irony. It was something to do with them having learned about her identity by combing through Veronica's phone messages. There was irony there, she was sure of it.

Give us the app. It was a gruff and chilling voice, but spoken with an old English eloquence. *Give me the app.* It had been repeated many times. *Give me the app.*

She will die… There had certainly been mentions of death. *I'll send you a finger for every…* Something. She couldn't remember what unit of time had been adjudged equal to a finger.

Annie reached for the bottle, but it was drained. The unpleasantness of the smell and the taste of her mouth were more evident to her now. She was still drunk, but not so drunk that she was numb, and reality dawned on her frighteningly.

She tried to stand. She stumbled a few paces then lowered herself to the ground again. As the minutes passed, her clarity improved, and all else in the world worsened. She began to consider the situation. She mulled the prospect of handing over the reins to Smith. It was the ultimate tool – hegemony from afar, a cocktail of control and anonymity.

She couldn't do it. But she had to do it. She had to save Veronica. Veronica was her truest friend. Why hadn't she been at the house? She must save Veronica. But how could she be sure of Smith's word? She thought vaguely of the police, but then she remembered Smith's promise to behead Veronica at even the faintest hint of a wailing siren.

She remembered also the perceived illegality of Pimple. She would have to comply with his wishes. There was nothing for it.

Then she was struck by a moment of clarity – a catholicon of the sort that can only be borne on hallucinatory quantities of alcohol.

Annie scrambled across the floor and hauled herself up to the table. She felt for her phone. She had it. She searched for the video message from Smith, making many wrong turns as her thumbs slid clumsily across the monitor. She had the video. She saved it. She was suddenly imbued with a certainty of purpose.

This was the answer. Perhaps it had always been the answer. There was a black humour in the fact that this was what it would all boil down to, and though she shook with fear, she was dismayed to feel the corners of her lips curling.

She rooted through the innards of the Pimple command centre on one of the open laptops, searching for the messaging boards. The Smith video – which so explicitly conveyed the nature of the situation – had arrived in her inbox. She heard the sound of its landing like the prodding of a far-off gong.

Annie's limp body slumped into a bare metal chair. Her drunkenness and her conviction sailed side by side in perfect equilibrium. Her thumb was poised. She pressed.

All over the capital, phones fizzed. Women glanced down to find an alert from Pimple, but this was no ordinary alert. It was the first thread on the forums to have ever been openly instigated by the app's creators; indeed, it was the first explicit sign of life, of any kind, from the creators themselves. Better yet, it was a video. Who could resist such an offering?

Users were drawn in by the thousand. Barely fifteen minutes later, an urgent general meeting of the app's user base had been called. Annie was by then unconscious.

PART IV

Enlightenment

The Tower

The station had a heartbeat, a low and regular thump that occasionally pulled together in a flowery riff. That came when the drummer chose to exhibit a little flair. The drummer himself was entirely anonymous, and yet omnipotent, like a noisy football god.

Chaos had descended outside the Tube station. Baker Street was riotous. A volcanic plane of white and red was rippling; a plume of red mist had just erupted on the other side of the road. A pub named The Globe was overrun with football fans, who were readying themselves for an evening game at Wembley.

'*Que sera, sera!*' they sang. They had formed ranks on either side of the road and in the central reservation. They were roaring madly at one another. One side would strike up a chant; the other answered.

Starting a chant was a special rite. Appearance was key. The balder, the more scarred, the grizzlier, the better. Tone of voice was also important – far more so than the decibel count, although that was important too. Hoarseness was the most obvious prerequisite; you had to be tuneful enough to rally support, but not so tuneful as to dampen it. It was a confusing business.

Policemen with plastic visors had encircled the fans like a semi-permeable cell membrane. A plucky man had lost his cool and was imitating a traffic warden, stopping and starting the oncoming cars with exaggerated gestures. He was quickly chivvied on by an angry officer, who seemed loathe to break rank. Crushed cans of lager were strewn all over. The tattoo ink ran thick.

The spoken obscenities were suffocating. Many of the chants – which at the outset seemed to be about football – inexplicably ended with a checklist of female erogenous zones. Fathers stood with ringed fingers resting on the shoulders of their awestruck sons.

They were all of a kin, they were all of them England fans; the chants were a constant reinforcement of that fact. In spite of this, the crowd carried the unmistakable air of threat. It was as if the singing of songs affirmed one's place amid the madness. Silence and serenity were to be treated with deep suspicion.

Annie managed to pass between the bodies unnoticed. Her head continued to ring as she emerged from the crowd. It was early evening, but the sun was bright and the air hot, and sweat was beading her brow. The pain in her head had all but pounded itself out, but still there was a slow thump – the feeling of blood on the move. It mirrored the dwindling heartbeat of the crowd as she moved further away.

The streets were now quite empty. The buildings on either side were tall, and for the most part residential. A few restaurants were dotted around, with their owners standing in front of them.

'Delicious curry this evening?' asked one as Annie passed.

'No, thank you,' she replied, with a nervous smile.

Then she glimpsed, for the first time, the form of a building under construction. It was a good deal loftier than its surroundings. All the streets were long and wide, laid out in a grid system, and so this taller structure could be seen from great distances, depending on the vantage point. It rose up against the dusk in Orwellian style.

Annie's trainers made no sound as she walked a few blocks closer. The building had a skeletal stone frame; its unfurnished floors were bared. It bulged in the middle from a narrower base, giving the effect of a ribcage rising from a slender waist. Glass stuck to the larger part of one of its sides like ice encroaching on a lake. The base was squared off by wooden walls that ran around its perimeter. These were plastered with the advertisements of a supposedly considerate construction company, and with warnings for potential intruders.

Annie positioned herself as close to these walls as she dared, sitting down beside a bus stop with a paper that she had bought. She looked to be reading as she waited for darkness to fall.

'People are going to get hurt,' panted Elena, as she struggled to keep up with Viola. 'You have to turn them around. They'll listen to you, Viola. They could die otherwise!'

Viola rounded on Elena, and the crowd surged forwards on either side of them. 'We may die today, Elena. I'm at peace with that.' She pointed a thick finger as she spoke. 'I'd rather die today fighting for the right to live freely, than to live my life on my back, blind, feeding off men who want only to exploit and abuse me.'

Women in the crowd had slowed to witness the exchange. Some voiced their support for Viola. She was drumming up quite a din.

'Men who want to work my flesh for gain. Men who would keep me in the dark, who would lock me away. Devils! The same men who have gone to the most unthinkable extremes to prevent us from seizing our freedom. Yes. Yes! I would die before ceding anything to *these* men.'

Viola tried to march on, but Elena blocked her. 'And would you have others die too?'

'All of us here would die for the same cause!' declared Viola. 'All of us.'

She had drawn her commanding frame right up close to Elena, who was slight by comparison.

Elena stood unwaveringly still. 'There has to be another way,' she said.

'Bah!' scoffed Viola, tossing her arms to the air and wheeling away.

She was dressed in an outfit of billowing whites, yellows and oranges. Her voluminous weave was stored up in a green bandana. When swirling she gave the impression of a tropical blancmange.

'To freedom!' she shouted, punching a fist.

The women around marched on, bouncing on their toes and cheering as they went. Some of them clutched beer cans. Elena was powerless to stop them. She followed because she felt that she must. Sasha was among them, but lost within the bodies.

Warren grimaced at the lifeless frame of his long-time friend and colleague, David Duffin. He was wrestling with that concoction of upset and anger that so often befalls those who learn of their betrayal only after the death of the traitor. Duffin's body had been discovered that afternoon by a member of the public. It had been poorly disguised, as if hidden in a hurry as a stopgap the previous evening. After positively identifying him, the timing of his demise had led Grace to call for an immediate review of his mobile phone activity; the results had proven disastrous.

The man Warren had known in life had not betrayed him. The David Duffin he had known had been a steadfast and loyal friend. He had depended on his counsel many times. They had cracked cases together, made arrests together, climbed through the ranks together. Their families had eaten together. But this man that lay greying on the floor was a different man entirely. Warren's knuckles whitened.

'What do we do?' It was Grace's voice. It seemed far away.

'There's nothing to do now,' said Warren.

'They must've had something on him, he would never have…'

'Don't,' he snapped.

He walked out of the warehouse and kicked a stray bucket that was rusting by the edge of the creek, roaring in frustration. He sat on a stout bollard and held a hand to his forehead. He scratched at a spot in the centre of his scalp that he scratched at whenever he worried. A tick had landed there when he was a boy, during a holiday in Canada. His father had discovered it after several hours, by which time it had swelled to the size of a small grape. His father knew to burn the beast to death with a boiling piece of cutlery before extracting it, but even the thought that its top half would have otherwise gone on burrowing was enough to leave an ineffaceable scar on Warren's imagination.

Men in white garments were scouring the scene around him for forensic evidence. Grace approached him cautiously.

'They have O'Mahony,' said Warren. 'I'm sure of it.'

It had been confirmed by a witness that there had been a commotion outside the home of Annie O'Mahony last night. A van had been seen screeching away. Police had arrived at the address less than an hour later, intending to make an arrest. The approximate timing of Duffin's death and the scuffle at O'Mahony's home had coincided, and

Warren felt sure he knew why. 'Smith wants the app. He's going to take control of it.'

'We won't let him do that,' said Grace defiantly.

Warren looked past her blankly. Grace sat down beside him. His mind revolved on the demise of David Duffin and he was filled with a feeling of great sadness, but it paled in relation to his anger.

A buzzing sound then emanated from Grace's pocket, reminding her of an unopened notification from Pimple. She pulled her phone out and clicked her tongue in annoyance. 'This bloody app!' she cried, making to stuff it back into her pocket.

Warren stopped her. 'What's it saying?' he demanded, his dark eyes suddenly alive.

'Just those forums.'

'Give it here.'

Grace handed the phone over. It took a matter of seconds for Warren to find the video that Annie O'Mahony had posted, the video in which a masked and muffled Emerson Smith laid out his intentions in explicit detail: to acquire control of the Pimple app through the ransoming of a woman named Veronica's life. Smith always had had a taste for the dramatic. Warren had long suspected that it might one day be his undoing.

Without speaking, Warren dashed for his nearby car. Grace started and went after him. There had been a subsequent meeting of the app's users – he had seen that messaging thread too. How had they been so blind as to stop monitoring the forums? How had they not anticipated Duffin's treachery? Now there was no time.

Emerson Smith stood with a leathery palm pressed flat against a stone column, gazing out into the glittering night. With his free hand, he pulled menacingly and contemplatively at his beard. His normally slicked hair was rather more ruffled than usual.

Veronica was lashed to a chair in the middle of the bone-bare floor. She was wearing nothing but a torn black dress, and her glasses were missing. Blood was drying on her chin and on the edges of her lips, and one of her eyes had been closed shut by bruising. Her hands were tied behind her back. She drew air raspingly through her nostrils.

Two of Smith's goons – 'Skinny' and John Canty – were stationed by the entrance to the raw stairwell. They were speaking in hushed tones. Lingering on the lower floors were two dozen thugs, all in the employ of Smith.

Veronica hadn't uttered a discernible word since her capture. She had stifled yelps of pain as best she could, and had so far managed to stem her tears and whimpers when evil threats were spat into her ears.

'You're going to die, Veronica. And your friend, Annie, she'll die too. And I shall have the app anyway.' Emerson spoke soullessly into the still night air.

The members of the Fist were scattered across the city. Bledi Shala, Reed McCoy, the Marques brothers from south London; each was awaiting an update from within their respective nests. Smith had not invited them to bear witness to the winning of the prize that was Pimple. Instead, he had arranged for men to be stationed outside each of their premises, and was poised to eradicate them.

He was so close. His masterstroke was at hand. Silent dominion beckoned, a dominion that he had no intention of sharing. At Smith's command, the men would massacre the Fist. But not yet. Soon he would create his power vacuum, but first he had to be sure that he could fill it.

'Veronica.' He turned to face her. 'I am very a reasonable man. But it takes two to be reasonable.'

He sat down on the spare chair so that he was facing his prey directly. Veronica looked away from him. His patience snapped. He seized her by the ears and yanked her head to face his. He looked demented, popping and contorting like water brought to boil.

'Give me the codes,' he hissed. 'Tell me where the mainframe is. Tell me how many users you have. Give me something, Veronica, anything, one tiny morsel of information. Give me something.'

Tears escaped Veronica's eyes as she whimpered in pain. She tried to turn away but he gripped her ears tightly. In a flash, Smith released an ear and flicked his fingers at Skinny, then grabbed the ear again. Skinny came up behind Veronica with a pair of pliers and fixed them to one of her fingers. She loosed a stoppered squeal and her eyes widened in otiose appeal. Smith released her ears, ran a hand across her forehead and brushed aside stray wisps of hair.

'Tell me something,' he said, softly. 'Veronica, you need to tell me something now.'

His commands rose in steady crescendo. Veronica made no perceptible motion of assent.

'Tell me!' he roared, his voice quaking.

He slapped her across the face. Veronica snapped her face back to his. She was flushed and choked and blood was flowing from her lips again, but there was a sunken determination to her appearance that drove Emerson wild. His left eye was twitching uncontrollably. After several seconds more of a mad, shared stare, he rose, spun, and clicked his fingers.

Skinny squeezed and violently twisted the pliers, breaking bone in Veronica's index finger and leaving it horribly misshapen. She let out a stifled, prolonged scream towards the stone ceiling which rebounded and reverberated, eventually dissipating into the outside air.

Smith had resumed his place by the building's edge, looking outwards like a hunched crow. He held his free hand aloft. Skinny latched the pliers' teeth around another violently shaking finger.

'Tell me something,' said Smith.

He heard no sound but the spluttering of pain. No attempt to talk. He clicked his fingers. He heard the cracking of bone, followed by another muted howl.

'Tell me,' he said again.

The same sequence ensued.

'Tell me.'

Once more, and again.

'Tell me.'

The rhythm of the struggle persisted.

The hulking figure of Benz rounded to face an approaching horde of women. He was tremendously wide as he reared, a solid slab of flesh; the men accompanying him were lost in his shadow.

Viola approached, ready to entreat with him. His slow brain looked to be working ferociously in an effort to comprehend the scene before him. Several hundred angry women or more had materialised, quite suddenly, as if unstitched from some parallel dimension. Annie was among them.

'We're here for Veronica,' said Viola assertively.

Benz was looking beyond her, eyes wide. He was clearly not used to being addressed so directly – certainly not by a member of the opposite sex. He appeared unnerved by the bright and prideful appearance of the woman.

'Don't know her. Best you move on, love,' he said.

Viola took another few steps forwards. 'We're here to take her back. Get out of the way.'

She took another step. Benz then cracked the back of his hand instinctively across her face and she fell soundlessly to the pavement. Several women surrounded and righted her. The crowd behind caught fire. There was a flurry of shouting and a general surge towards the entrance to the building site. Benz – whose highly conditioned brain had failed to grasp that his nervousness was born of fear – looked suddenly panicked.

The women were converging. His comrades were on their feet beside him, hoods raised. Benz reached for his waist. The entrance way was barred. Firearms were brandished. Some of the frontline women fingered shivs, hammers, and other improvised weaponry.

'Let us through,' bellowed Viola above the rising din, shunting her weight backwards into the crowd in an effort to restrain its advance. 'There needn't be violence here.'

Benz and the other men kept their weapons aloft. With the crowd's advance paused, Viola stepped slowly into the narrowing no-man's land of dust-track that still separated the two sides – the old and the new.

Then, from on high, came a woman's cry, almost lost in the distance between the rafters and ground level. Annie recognised it and her stomach lurched. Women further back, energised and enraged by the noise, threw themselves forwards, nudging the crowd on so that like a mudslide it spilled over into the compound.

A frenzied mêlée ensued. The men, much to Annie's amazement, seemed not to be able bring themselves to fire. The women, rather than hacking and stabbing like crazed jackals, thumped at the men with the hilts of their hammers or clambered on them in numbers and dragged them to the floor. The men were swiftly and for the most part painlessly overrun. Women went marauding in packs into the building site, feeding off adrenaline as they swarmed.

Annie glimpsed Viola's dust-covered form to one side, straddling the pinioned and crooked form of Benz, who was laid out on his back. Her left hand was clamped to one bulky trapezius – bulked, perhaps, by his lifetime of indifference. Her other hand held a switchblade up against his throat.

'Don't you dare move,' she warned.

'What the fuck is happening down there? John? John!' The building shook and Emerson fell back from its edge. 'John!' The line had gone dead. 'Skinny!'

Skinny, who was loitering by Veronica, snapped to attention.

'Get down there and find out what the fuck is going on.'

Veronica was still tied to the chair. Her head was lolling slightly to one side. She was flitting in and out of consciousness. Sporadically she glanced towards the stairwell, as if faintly aware of the fracas downstairs. Smith peered through faded eyes at the crowds down below. He had long needed spectacles but had never wanted to wear them; even so, he could just make out the bobbing heads of a teeming horde of women. He turned on his heel and marched up to Veronica and breathed into her face.

'Who are these people on my doorstep, eh?' he demanded. 'Who are they? They're your fucking whores, aren't they! They're going to die too, Veronica. Look what you've done now!'

He shook the frame of the chair maniacally. Veronica's head jangled like a doll's. Smith stilled the chair. He was hyperventilating. He began to pace the floor, muttering to himself. He tried to flatten his hair against his scalp but it remained stubbornly dishevelled. His composure had dwindled to nothing.

'John?' said Emerson, frantically answering his phone. 'Tom? What the fuck do you want? Are you in position?' There was a pause while he waited for the reply. 'I don't care what he says, Tom, don't you move another fucking muscle till I say so, you hear me? Not a fucking muscle.' His distress seemed to have intensified. Another pause. 'You're not to touch the girls, remember. Do not touch the girls. Make sure they get away – and make sure the others do the same. Target only the pimps, you hear me? Only the pimps. Wait for my call.'

Suddenly, the commotion downstairs sounded nearer, and Emerson started in alarm. He buttoned up his blazer, sat down on a steel girder and tried to think through the situation, clasping his hands together tightly.

There was no way down. He could go no further up. Victory or defeat was at hand, but he couldn't tell which. He wished then that the floors were made of glass, so that he could gauge the progress of his men downstairs.

Elena moved with a pinched-off pocket of the crowd into the shadow of the towering building. The sky was alive with the racket of conflict. The dust and dirt on the ground had been whipped up into plumes around her.

She passed inside, and the noise intensified. Defeated women were staggering out in ones and twos: disorientated, deafened, some supporting each other. Some looked totally lost. The women that rushed by them in the opposite direction moved in packs. Some carried makeshift smoke-grenades; Elena had seen several women throw these into the structure from the outside. The insides were dense with smoke. All was confusion.

Elena felt her way upwards to find wounded women slumped against the walls. Several men had been sedated and were being watched over by grim-faced women. Often there were discarded guns nearby that didn't seem to have been fired. It may have been clear-cut war for Emerson Smith, but not for his men. Not all of them anyway. They had families, and, in some cases, at least a few shreds of compassion.

Elena moved through the smoke and knelt by the side of a young girl of no more than twenty years old, helping her to stem a gash at her neck by tearing off a piece of her own sleeve. She then climbed further, arm out in front of her, and the racket grew. She was in among the bodies once more – but most of these appeared to be female.

Another floor. A few people here were grappling wildly, stumbling through the mist. A fat man fell over backwards into Elena's line of sight, and reached for a rifle that was lying on the floor beside him. He struggled to sit up, then took aim at an emerging woman with an unruly tangle of hair.

'Look out!' cried Elena, but her words were lost as a loud crash sounded overhead. Somehow the weapon failed to fire. The man, still seated in the chaos, inspected the weapon with dazed curiosity. He then got ready to fire once more.

Elena ran at him and launched her full weight at the side of his head, shoulder first. He squeezed the trigger and fired through a parting in the smoke, out into the open.

Elena was on top of him, hammering with her fists. He caught hold of a wrist and rolled her over, yanking a knife from his belt. He raised it up theatrically high. His mouth was open. He might well have been roaring.

In near death, Elena didn't witness a show-reel of her life's most significant moments. Instead she noted, with total clarity, the thick plaque on his teeth, and the gold in his molars. He was among the worst of them, rotten on the inside. She would never forget his mouth, that rotten mouth, which opened onto death.

But before the knife could fall, another woman had hurled herself into his spine. He fell to one side, convulsing. The curly-haired woman with raking blue eyes had replaced him.

Elena recognised her. She seemed to recognise Elena. They shared a split-second connection in which much was assumed. Then three bodies fell across them, and they scrambled separate ways. Elena continued to climb.

The sound of the sirens rose and fell like the turning of a lighthouse beacon. The cars ahead folded to one side as best they could. Warren blew past red lights and through numerous complex junctions. Much of the city was still, but those who were still out snapped to attention as the car shot by them. Grace gripped the sides of her seat in fear. Warren drove like a man possessed, like a man on the trail of a singularly elusive treasure – the kind that evades capture long enough to mutate into a debilitating and insatiable obsession.

'Careful, Warren!' warned Grace, as they swung around another corner at breakneck speed. The street lights were all merging into one. An armada of local policemen would likely be arriving at the location any second; Warren had to be on hand to guide them. There were certain individuals who must not be allowed to wriggle free. *Never again*, he thought – or he may have said it aloud, for Grace flashed her widened eyes towards him.

'All units, be advised. Gunfire on Camelot Road. Proceed with caution,' announced the car's radio system.

Again he felt Grace turn to face him, nervously, but he had hardly registered the update. He had expected gunfire. In truth he was surprised that it hadn't been described as heavy, and that caution alone had been advised.

This was it: the coming to a head of years of patience and subtle manoeuvring. It was all he could think of. His mind was a melting pot of fear and focus. It was now very late, verging on early, but he didn't feel fatigue, or temperature, he thought nothing of family or money or anything else at all. He thought only of one end, and he lashed the creaking vehicle on into the night.

Emerson arose from his perch and made straight for Veronica, determined to take one last run at her. He was becoming desperate.

The din from below was approaching. Veronica's head was hanging slackly to one side. She appeared to be in a state of near-sleep. A flood of tears had dried on her face and upper chest. Emerson swung his body down in front of hers and pulled at her chin, assuming that he would be met with the same, obdurate silence.

'No,' she whimpered. Her eyes opened and met with his. He saw, for the first time, the seeds of submission. 'Please, no more.'

Fresh tears were rolling towards their dried predecessors.

Emerson coiled like a snake. 'You know what you have to do,

Veronica.' She tried to look away, but he wouldn't let her. 'Give me the app.'

Veronica wore a determined look, just as she had throughout her captivity, only now it was – for the first time – somewhat withered.

'I can't,' she said, in a trembling voice.

Smith rose and retrieved the pliers. He held them up against Veronica's face. 'I will pluck the teeth from your skull unless you tell me.' He moved the open pliers towards her mouth, as if preparing to feed an infant.

'No!' said Veronica, shuddering with fear. 'I'll tell you! Please.'

'Then tell me now!' he yelled.

Veronica panted as she tried to compose herself to the point that she could speak. 'I'll take you to the control room,' she said, wrecked and disconsolate, the power gone from her voice. 'We run the app from a hub right here in London. I'll give you the codes to the mainframe. Just get me out of here.'

'We're going right now,' said Emerson, rising to his feet and slashing Veronica's ties. He pulled her slight frame into his and whispered menacingly into her ear, 'If I suspect you of misleading me, I'll kill you. I'll kill your family, your friends, your friends' friends and their children. I'll enslave every person you ever knew and every woman that ever used the fucking app. I'll erase everything you are.'

Veronica, cowering, made one last plea. 'Promise me one thing,' she said, with renewed strength. 'Promise me that you won't harm Annie. You must promise me that.'

Emerson met her stare, considering. 'You have my word,' he said.

His phone chirped from his pocket. A question mark was waiting in an unread message. Veronica risked an imperceptible downward glance. Emerson was temporarily lost as to what to do next. But in his desperation, he convinced himself that Veronica's will had truly been broken, and the plan could proceed. He replied with a single word: *Go.*

A swarm of warring bodies buffeted Annie this way and that. She ducked as a hulking figure went charging by. Men were being harangued by scores of women. Like drunken trolls, they were swinging and kicking at all that moved. One such man, his perimeter breached, was sinking slowly to the floor, drained beneath a flurry of hands. A stout, spherical shape had managed to clear a space and was brandishing a steel pipe. Blood lifted into the air around him like sea spray. But the space soon caved in, and the figure was swallowed up.

And then came a moment, a crystallising moment in which an infinitesimally exact set of circumstances came to a head. Annie had never experienced anything like it, and never would again. The bedlam around her seemed to slow, almost to a total halt. The spinning of the world seemed to stop. War was being waged on every side. Fists and feet and all kinds of makeshift weaponry were raised. A tooth was suspended mid-air. Blood was oozing, lives were on the line, and not only in that moment, but in moments yet to pass. Past lives that had been staked and lost on similar causes weighed also on the scene. The stage itself appeared to melt, slow as wax at first, then steadily, like blood, then fast as water spouting from a glacial tongue.

Annie's surroundings morphed into a great and raging river that stretched backwards through millennia and flowed unendingly ahead. There were people in the river. Many were struggling against the current, others were simply being borne along. Veronica and Peter Froome were in the river, and her ex-husband Oliver and Emerson Smith and Rory de Sansa and the prostitute Elena. There were hundreds and hundreds of women and men. There were all kinds of faces, old and new. It seemed not to matter whether they struggled, or over what they were struggling, or for what reasons, or the righteousness of those reasons, for they were each of them bound to go the way of the river in the end. Annie was freed of all feeling.

The world then glimmered into view once more, faintly at first. As if falling against a bed of black tiles, the river seemed to sizzle and then angrily began ceding its component parts. A grappling man and woman were the first to resurface, still coated in a watery film. Then more bodies came. Then the bare bones of the building. The river's residual matter gathered form as more and more water evaporated. Then the moment ended.

The battle was set to encroach upon the uppermost floor of the building. Emerson Smith moved cautiously down the staircase, down into the thinning fog. He peeked around the corner.

Several women were draped across a staggering man – it may have been Marsden – who was flailing at them madly. He managed to free himself from one, throwing her headlong into the wall. But then the other two, both of them red-headed, were at him. One had her arm tied tight around his neck, and he didn't have a free hand left to fend her off with.

Emerson took another step, as if to enter into the fray. Then he recoiled at a loud clanging of metal from below. He scurried back up the stairs, like a rat escaping from a swiftly sinking ship. He was not a coward. He had instigated and been embroiled in a great many fights in his time, armed and otherwise. Only now he had something to lose – an immeasurably precious thing. There could be no risks.

A frenzy of thought electrified his mind. There was no way down, and no way up. The women looked to have gained the upper hand, though he could barely believe it. They would be on him in minutes. He had hardly heard a weapon fired. He had to move now.

'Get up!' he shouted. 'Get up!'

Veronica's eyes were closed. Her head continued to roll from side to side. Smith hauled her to her feet once more. She groaned. There was no strength left in her legs. Her broken fingers prevented her from grabbing hold of him for support.

Smith propped her up as if he were a field medic. Together they grunted their way to the stairwell. Smith gripped a pistol in his free hand. His shirt had three too many buttons undone. His dark brown hair was still ruffled and bubbles of sweat were clinging to his face. Veronica limped alongside him like a blind drunk. There was a cacophony of confused shouting below.

'Are you OK? Lisa?'

'Down!'

'Get her!'

'Look there, behind there!'

'Where are the others? Where's Lisa?'

Erratic, jumbled up words were barked, and the rattling echoes of hurried footsteps rained. Now, in among those sounds, were sirens – a far-off undercurrent of sirens.

Veronica was waking up again. Her feet were being dragged across the dusty floor, and the cold kiss of the pistol was at her neck. She began to resist, digging her heels into the floor with what power she had left. Smith hauled her on and thumped her on the shoulder. Her eyelids lifted heavily and she scanned the smoky scene.

'Help,' she croaked. 'Help me.'

The words dissolved into the throng.

'Help me!' she tried again, with greater zest.

A woman with sleek dark hair was crouching nearby and spied them through the fog. Smith brushed the gun against Veronica's forehead, warning against interference. The struggle here was still fierce enough that he could move beneath it, kicking and swiping at impeding bodies as he went, and ducking down behind the piles of bricks and timber. They made it down a flight of stairs. Here they were forced to cross an open floor in order to descend further. The dark and the smoke gave them cover.

On this floor the conflict had dwindled. There were no men left to resist the women. Some men lay on their fronts with their hands ziplocked behind their backs like trussed turkeys. Women were nursing their wounds and hurrying back and forth, or wandering around dazed. In the middle of that bare expanse, Smith was exposed. He kept to the perimeter, hoping in vain to blend into the night sky. Women had begun to trail him, warily.

'Give her over, now.' Sasha approached them, a gun trained on Smith.

'Get back!' Smith fired a shot into the ceiling. 'The next one's in her fucking head!'

The woman with the perennially creased forehead – Sadie – was circling too, with two or three others, like a pack of wolves closing in on wounded prey. Smith paced backwards across the floor, facing Veronica to his pursuers. The discarded, almost entirely unused weapons of his defeated men now tracked his twitching muscles.

'Not another fucking step,' he hissed, widening the berth between himself and the women, waving the pistol at Veronica's temple. The stairs were within his reach.

Annie O'Mahony's face then surfaced among the onlookers. Her heart sank when she saw her friend and she swallowed the urge to cry out. Their eyes met: a terrible, wrenching linkage. Annie was filled with the densest blend of grief and guilt and fear; although she also felt, through it all, that Veronica was trying to convey a message to her.

The women, still growing in number, enclosed Smith and Veronica within a semi-circle, cutting off their passage to the stairs.

'You... You fucking ingrates...' he wheezed. His eyes glinted through the darkness. 'I raised you. I raised you! And I have defended you... Been a father to you. What will you do without me? Without us?'

He began to cackle. All the while he was creeping like a crab towards the stairwell, just a few feet from the building's edge. The women shifted reluctantly to accommodate his advance, mindful of the gun that was still trained on Veronica's forehead.

'What will you do?' he yelled again. 'Things are... like this... for a reason. It's change that's backwards. It's change that divides us, that leads to this!' He gestured around him. 'This is just a cycle. You watch... You watch what your beloved Pimple becomes.' He then lurched more determinedly at the women. 'Out of my way.'

The bodies would not yield for him.

'Out of my damn way!'

Then he caught sight of Elena, standing among them.

'You!' he cried, his face crinkling in disgust. 'You!' he said again. 'You...' he continued, as if furiously searching for the perfect descriptor.

He had lost his focus. Annie and Veronica had not broken eye contact. Veronica now widened her eyes, and her body, which had been wholly limp, suddenly stiffened in Emerson's grasp.

'Make it worth something,' said Veronica weakly.

And with that, she bent at the knees and thrust herself upwards. The crown of her head struck Emerson's chin and caused his teeth to crash together, splintering chips from the front two. His lean body ricocheted backwards. With one arm he continued to hug Veronica at the waist. He pulled her tighter still, in the hope that she might act as an anchor. With the other arm he waved the pistol wildly, but was too unbalanced to fire it.

The first of his falling feet failed to touch the ground and instead slipped over the precipice. The second found the lip of the building, but not enough of it. And so Emerson Smith tumbled, screaming and flailing, into the night air. Veronica, no longer strong enough to resist, went with him.

Together they fell, facing separate ways, inches apart. Annie heard cries of anguish rising up, but no clearer note among them – no note belonging to her friend. She could almost hear the rush of the air flying past her delicate frame, but no cries of fear. Annie was nigh unconscious, dizzied, as she rushed forwards to the building's lip: too late to see the bodies airborne.

In the nightmares of years to come, Annie would be beset by the phrase 'fall guy'. There always has to be a fall guy, she would observe, on an unending loop: somebody to bear the brunt of the bad times, that there might be good again. It was never meant to be Veronica.

The sirens were close now, as if signalling the end of days. They were just around the corner. The women began to pour from the structure like termites from a drowned nest.

Warren was on the tails of the local law enforcers by the time they arrived at the scene. Pandemonium erupted only moments later. The officers, heavily armed and armoured, were preparing to storm the site. Warren, wearing the long, dark overcoat he wore every day, stood in their midst, barking orders, outlining priorities. A number of stray women had already been subdued and arrested, as had a lone man, who was bleeding from the ear.

Suddenly, in much the way that they had spilled over into the compound in the first place, a dustier and grimmer-looking collection of women exploded from within. They poured through the fencing cracks and through the doors and scrambled over the enclosure top.

'Hold fire!' bellowed Warren. 'Hold fire! Round 'em up!'

Policemen scattered this way and that, pursuing the women in clusters in the darkness. Some women were too weak to flee and simply gave themselves up. The officers seemed not to know how to treat their captives; handcuffs were gingerly placed on some, but other bloodstained women were softly chaperoned towards the open backs of vans. It was an apt encapsulation of the moral quandaries coughed up by Pimple: were these the victims, or the villains? Either way, the police could not possibly hope to contain the droves of women who continued to flow out of the compound.

Warren pushed frantically past the bodies. The building site was quickly emptying as he headed around the perimeter of the building. Women gave him a wide berth as they fled, but he paid them no mind.

Then he stopped. On his left, laid on its back, was the disfigured but clearly recognisable corpse of Emerson Smith. One side of his face had been so brutally crumpled that it was now little more than fallen flesh. A pile of steel beams to one side bore a smattering of blood. His face, though grotesquely caved in, was painted still in the colours of indignation. A slim, dark-haired woman lay motionless by his side. She bore none of the marks of impact, but Warren was sure that she was dead. He touched his fingers to her neck to be certain. There was no pulse.

Warren looked away from the pair, stifling the urge to cry out. Slower women continued to drain from the building around him and he supposed that he had better waylay them, but he hadn't the heart.

Then, in a far-off corner of the compound, he saw a lone woman weaving towards an exit of sorts. Women were hopping from a barrel onto an industrial crate and out over the fence. But this particular woman was staggering around, disorientated. Her tangled thicket of hair was distinctive even at a distance, even in the darkness.

Warren knew at once who she was. He set off at a gallop in her direction, just as she clambered up onto the container. She saw him coming, and dropped hastily from sight.

'Veronica. Veronica, I'm so sorry. Veronica.'

The weight of Annie's friend had become too much for her. She had stopped in a gap between two buildings a short distance from the construction site and propped herself up against a wall behind a skip.

Grief shook her to the core. Her voice had cracked. Tears had matted hair against her cheeks. She tilted her neck back and looked up to the heavens, closing her eyes as tightly as she could, hoping the world would fold in on itself; from her mouth came quiet, drawn-out sounds of misery.

'We need to…' said Annie. 'We need…'

She was trying to coax the ghost of her friend upright with soft movements, but Veronica waved them off. Annie persisted. Then Veronica's shimmering form came suddenly and sharply into focus.

Make it worth something, she had said. Annie remembered now. Had she truly meant it? Veronica, who had turned her back on the app? Who had denounced it? Annie felt sick for even considering this. Shame and sadness swallowed her up again. For perhaps the first time she contemplated how silly it all was – that so much pain, suffering and upheaval should have arisen over a mobile app. Pixels on a screen: what a wasted cause they seemed. But though she was a long way from fully comprehending it, Annie had now been bound till death to that same cause. Bound to give all she had to making a success of the app, and in a way that Veronica would have approved of. There was no other way for her to live; Veronica's martyrdom had seen to it.

'We meet at last.'

A gruff voice penetrated her misery. The air between them was charged. Neither moved a muscle.

'Or should I say again, Miss O'Mahony.' Warren was panting as he spoke. 'I've come to arrest you,' he announced, feeling rather strange as he did so.

Annie hadn't the strength to run away, nor the will. She flailed her arm helplessly, spluttering through tears. 'On what grounds?'

'Racketeering,' said Warren, untucking a set of handcuffs from his inside coat pocket. 'Pimping.'

'And who have I pimped, exactly?' flared Annie.

The banality of the exchange – set within the shadow of that bloody, unfinished building – seemed momentarily lost on them both.

'I've met many of them,' grunted Warren in reply. 'One looked a great deal like you, in fact. And there are many thousands more.' He seemed to be reassuring himself as much as telling her. The handcuffs still dangled from his fingers, unused.

She became emboldened by his apparent reluctance to act. 'I think you're mistaking me for the men back there.'

She pointed towards the building. She didn't care so much about her freedom as she did the need to be free. Her freedom was paramount to the enactment of Veronica's last instruction.

'Their blood is on your hands too,' said Warren.

The intonation of the sentence was perplexing. Annie cocked her head to one side scornfully, and sniffled aggressively. 'Ask yourself what happened here, truly.'

Sirens cried out around the corner; Warren jangled the cuffs.

'You seem just strange enough to trust,' said Annie, grabbing a fistful of his coat. 'And it's not as though I have much choice in the matter. You're right. I built Pimple. Pimple makes prostitution safer, more transparent, more lucrative, and more damn modern. All the money that's been made has been spent on maintaining the app. The problems that it's had have been caused by the very men that it rendered impotent. Those men are right now fading from relevance and memory! Their sun is setting. And now we have a chance to plug up the gap they leave behind, with a fancy bit of tech and whole lot of grit. And mark my words, there'll be others if we don't. We've got one chance,' she finished, tugging him closer, forcing him to look her in the eye.

She held Warren in a vice for what seemed like minutes. A technicolour tide rippled across his eyes: scattered objects left askew, pain met with anger, Emerson Smith arisen. When he walked away, it was without a sound. He may have nodded; he wasn't sure. He gently swiped aside her hand. His every movement flowed suddenly from a font without source. He walked in a daze.

It was only later, when Warren rejoined Grace, who had feared for his safety, that he realised he had left his handcuffs behind.

Annie's pain would never leave her, of that much she was certain. It would rumble away beneath her feet as though it were the very furnace at the heart of the earth, far off and softened through the crust, but omnipotent nonetheless. No matter where she went or what she did in the world, that same pain would lurk, just as far off as before, every bit as inextinguishable, too deep-rooted to silence. It would pull on her until the day she died, when finally it would succeed in dragging her a few feet deep. Till then, it would marshal her thoughts, anchor her resolve, and keep her scattered life in line.

She walked until she could walk no further. She walked until her weariness had worn away at her grief, till her footsteps had, by the slimmest of margins, dulled the stinging of her loss. Ribbons of deep blue were showing in the sky as the sun neared the summit of the world. She hailed herself an Uber.

There was, as ever there is, work to be done.

Once inside the taxi, Annie fell instantly into a deep and lustrous dream. It was a dream that was rooted in innovation. It was about the amelioration of the lives of humankind, about the application of technology, about all the things that Annie lived and burned for. Only there were no prostitutes, no pimps, no sex and no Veronica. When she returned to consciousness, she fumbled after the threads of the dream, but could only anchor a few, while the others floated away.

What she clung to was hazy, but as she strained, she half-remembered: she had dreamed of a technological fix for homelessness.

Acknowledgements

My most heartfelt thanks go to Christine and Mark Weeks, for their invaluable efforts in helping to bring this project to fruition; to Unbound, without which it may never have happened; and to all those who pledged to support the *Pimple* campaign online. Words cannot express how grateful I am for the opportunity.

Patrons

Gazel Algan
Maddie Billings
Amber Billings
Allyson Calveley
Max Chee
Julian Cork
Florence Cornwell
Elle
John Goodall
Marsili Hale
Johari Ismail
Sebastian Ives
Susanna Kindler
Natalie Leyhane
Will Markiewicz
Nigel Ransom
Ben Smeaton
Jo Stanyard
Richard Steventon
James Tall
Georgette Taylor
Olivia Volk
Kristian Walesby
Darren Westlaek
Hannah Williams
Mike Williams
Isobel Wood
Tyler Woollard

'... The machinery had lacked a certain level of sophistication, hence Mr Omuro's undoing. But the site had also lacked what Annie described as 'Uberisation'. The lewd advertisements were static and the matchmakings were not facilitated in a timely fashion. RedBook could not bring together two souls at the very point of need. But Pimple could...'